NEW DIRECTIONS 49

In memoriam

ROBERT FITZGERALD
1910–1985

COLEMAN DOWELL
1925–1985

N D

New Directions in Prose and Poetry 49

Edited by J. Laughlin

with Peter Glassgold and Elizabeth Harper

A New Directions Book

Library of Congress Catalog Card Number: 37–1751

ACKNOWLEDGMENTS
Grateful acknowledgment is made to the editors and publishers of magazines in which some of the material in this volume first appeared: for Sally Fisher, *Field;* for Oscar Mandel, *The Dalhousie Review;* for Carl Rakosi, *Exquisite Corpse;* for Eliot Weinberger, *Sagetrieb.*

Maxine Chernoff's "Five Prose Poems" were included in her collection *New Faces of 1952* (Copyright © 1985 by Maxine Chernoff), published by Ithaca House, 108 North Plain Street, Ithaca, New York 14850.

"Everyone Knows Somebody Who's Dead," by B. S. Johnson, is taken from his collection *Aren't You Rather Young to Be Writing Your Memoirs?* (Copyright © 1972, 1973 by B. S. Johnson), published in 1973 by Hutchinson & Co., Ltd., London.

The quotations in Michael McClure's "April Arboretum" are taken from *Hierarchy: Perspectives for Ecological Complexity* by T. F. H. Allen and Thomas B. Starr (Copyright © 1982 by The University of Chicago Press).

"Saint Erkenwald," by Omar S. Pound (Copyright © 1984 by Omar S. Pound), was first published as a signed, limited edition by Woolmer/Brotherson Ltd., Revere, Pennsylvania 18953.

Howard Stern's "Variations on a Heliotrope of Rainer Maria Rilke" were included in a *Festschrift for René Wellek,* published in 1984 by Verlag Peter Lang AG, Bern, Switzerland.

The poems quoted on pages 181 and 182, in Eliot Weinberger's "At the Death of Kenneth Rexroth," can be found in *The Morning Star* (Copyright © 1979 by Kenneth Rexroth) and *The Complete Poems of Li Ch'ing-chao* (Copyright © 1979 by Kenneth Rexroth and Ling Chung), both published by New Directions.

Manufactured in the United States of America
First published clothbound (ISBN: 0–8112–0967–9) and as New Directions Paperbook 609 (ISBN: 0–8112–0968–7) in 1985
Published in Canada by Penguin Books Canada Limited

New Directions Books are published for James Laughlin
by New Directions Publishing Corporation,
80 Eighth Avenue, New York 10011

CONTENTS

APRIL ARBORETUM

MICHAEL McCLURE

For Kenneth Rexroth

1

THE KILLDEER CRIES CEASELESSLY IN THIS
MANICURED NATURE
and the dark brown molehills gloat with their life.
The book in hand states
that an earlier chapter,
"has identified an intensified
capacity for anticipation
as an important characteristic
of life
that sets it apart
from a dead matrix."
Inertness is a possibility of life
when it reaches deep
into the substrate.
THE LIVING
creates that which is less
alive
to carry it, to preserve it, to float it.
Poems are notes
written down

to obliterate
the shimmering,
to bring one into
agnosia of blackness.
((This is one way that we awake from our dreams.))

Grackles stride
over conglomerate pavement
and peer through the heap
of pruned branches
with glint-yellow eyes
that see nothing:
their consciousness
is a contretemps,
as innocent as a haiku
abandoning form
in mimesis of imagined experience.
Slush-slush-slush, whip-
whip-whip, whirr-whirr-
whirr, say the sprinklers
and the truck roar
looms leeward over the cypresses.
The abandoned coke bottle
is information if
it affects the future
but that is the business
of the future
which, says Whitehead,
is to be dangerous.
Always I die in the present
as I seek in the dense
phantom future.
". . . the evolutionary process
that has brought anticipation
to a critical level in living
systems also occurs
in the abiotic world."
The three band-tailed pigeons
flying over will tap their beaks

on the earth.
The mass of pink and white blossoms
will always be there
by the pattern of daisies.

Walking on I find a swan preening, rubbing looped neck against crop, under a white rhododendron in mix of sun and shade. A hen goose hobbles over and bites my pants leg and boot and then settles down by my foot. Turtles jump from a log into the pond. Mallards and their chicks paddle in the dark water. A heavy brown rabbit disappears into the tangle. A sky-blue and shark-blue jay in the herb garden is fine as the lilac-breasted roller of Africa. The sun of April morning drives cobwebs from my back. There are rainbows in the sprinklers under the redwoods and eucalyptuses. I am sampling the thyme and sage and rosemary and picking lavender to press in my notebook.

2

ALL OF NATURE IS NOT SUFFICIENT
FOR GREED
and we twist nature, turn
it, shape it—making exquisite
gardens to preserve it. Greed
wishes to feed upon
itself without losing
the source. The scrub jay
might be grateful if he knew
for he perceives that even
greed is ebullient, is reason.
He strides over the hillside stones
carefully placed there
where a brook runs watering
the thyme, the lavender
and hellebore. He's the state
of his hungers—avian pride—
bristling and bedecked
in appetitive emotions,
blue-flash, gray-blue
and

HUGE,
monumental in the flickering
of visceral myths through
immeasurable muscles.
He's larger than any star
AND HE'S HERE
with twitch of eye and glittering crown.

On the hill by the hospital
stands a sculpture
of a bear, simplified
as the garden simplifies
wilderness and brings exotic herbs,
bristlecones and giant ferns. Once there
were sand dunes here
and butterflies in abundance pumping
mooned wings in the April
sun. (A grizzly
ambled to the ocean
to feast on sea elephant corpses.)
Now I'm in
this whirligig
of blossoming mauve rhododendrons
and massive purple branches
of Oregon grape
cultivated
for their beauty and not their
succulence.
EVEN
THIS
IS
GREED,
as I am greed-embodied
and thereby immortal.
Not even *nothing* is enough!
NOT EVEN BLACKNESS OR ITS IMAGES
SAVE ME!
The jay picks up a crumb,
flies near and inserts

it into the humus,
steps closer, tilts his head
and stares with dark eye!
He creates an Osirian
recycling of remembrances
for worms, nematodes and beetles.
Sunlight brightens the page
to a white glare,
"The boundary surface for one property
(such as heat flow) will tend to coincide
with the boundary surfaces for many other
properties (such as blood flow, sensory
endings, physical density, and so on)
because the surfaces are mutually
reinforcing . . . This is what makes
a collection of properties
a *thing*
rather than a smear of overlapping
images."

Almost
invisible
color
prisms
at
the edge
of
the page.

The bookmark is a postcard panorama
of a Kenyan waterhole where a herd
of zebras intermixes with wildebeeste.
Many stand in the pool
up to their chins drinking; others
are alert, heads lifted and watching.
The ripplings of the gray-blue water
would be the shimmering surface
of a jewel if seen from the air.
There are slender thorn acacias
in the background and a distant
spur of Serengeti hills.
Now
a pigeon awkwardly
lands, flurrying his wings
as his toes reach out. —A flash of gray
and iridescence at the corner of my eye!
The bird could be eaten after a course
of raw oysters and a light salad.

3
THE DETRITUS OF JOY!

On the white tile men's room wall, the graffito:
NANCY REAGAN SLEPT HERE,
in dark blue felt tip pen.

The garbage can
holds waxboard cup for milkshakes,
kleenex spotted with makeup, empty
club soda bottle, paper bags, red and white
Winston carton and box
for Chinese food. It is full as I am.
The surface of the pond wobbles
beaming a deep brownish-gray. A drake
stands on the rock, half-alert,
with green shining head and orange feet.
Two heavy blond
women stop running
and point at him. He drops
into the water where
his reflection
had been
an instant before.
As the spray of the sprinkler
passes the dwarf red bamboo
a rainbow expands and shimmers.
The momentary site
eliminates proportion and sets
consciousness free. (I am filled
with detritus of joy.)
A pigeon alights on the rock,
bends forward to drink—sips—
and flies to the mottle of light.
The four pigeons picking there
have no interest in the squirrel
whose skinny ribcase
resembles that of a slender
nine year old boy. There is a pair

of top-knotted quail
under the evergreens.
Their toes crackle
in the fallen leaves;
the cock pecks at a blown azalea flower.
As they scratch, the cock's
black mask swivels
drawn by blank curiosity.

Crumbs of cracked corn
have been thrown here
for everyone.
"TO A WISE MAN
GOOD AND BAD LUCK
ARE LIKE HIS LEFT AND RIGHT HAND
HE USES BOTH,"
is
another
graffito
in the men's room.
It is attributed to St. Catherine.
Luck is detritus
of joy—both good and bad luck
like pride and hurt pride.
From boughs on high the squirrel
makes his alarm call, *Koo-ka-ka!*
Whoo-ka-ka!
"The cacti experience drought
as the normal state of affairs. Ephemerals,
which appear after the frequent rains,
complete their life cycle so rapidly
that they never experience the drought,"
states the caption under the photo
of an Arizona desert scene.

THE NEWS

INGEBORG DREWITZ

Translated from the German by Claudia Johnson

A morning in November, a typical morning. Children ride or walk to school. Men and women ride or walk to work. The lights stay on in the subway cars, even during the stretches above ground, the buses have their lights on, car headlights pair off into meandering, gliding chains of light, the street lights haven't been turned off yet. In the evening, after work, they'll be turned on again, car headlights will pair off again into meandering, gliding chains of light, the buses will have their lights on again, and the lights will stay on in the subway cars again, even during the stretches above ground, fluorescent white, incandescent yellow, and also the colorful neon signs.

Like everyone else, the children, the men and women, Eberhard W.—office employee, had grown accustomed to the way things are, grown used to the fact that from November to February, daytime remains outside his office window (except for weekends and other days off). He's standing with his back to a partition on the side of the subway car facing away from the platform, no smoking, a spot which no one else competes for, naturally all the seats are taken and the children don't stand up, even the handicapped have to show their I.D.'s (*reverentia cane capitis*, who remembers that, who abides by it?), a spot for watching people getting on and off, people he knows, since they always ride the same train he does, and yet people he doesn't really know, tired faces, pale faces, bad teeth when they smile on Friday evening or on the last day of work before Christmas.

He still has twelve years to go before he retires, has thirty-six years of service behind him, including his apprenticeship and the war. Thanks to his age, he's worked his way up by now to four weeks' vacation a year, a passable amount of free time if you add in weekends and religious holidays. When the New Year's Eve show comes on television, he thinks about vacation time, about bright evenings and open skies, about raging streams and reed-choked banks, about white-washed houses with low-hanging roofs, about grasshoppers screeching, and shimmering curtains, about men and women mending fishing nets, about barefoot girls licking ice-cream cones, six or seven years old. Back when his own two were that age, he'd felt on top of the world. Made them happy with an ice-cream cone, picked blueberries with them during vacation, let them ride the merry-go-round and taught them how to swim. And when his wife put them to bed, the smell of summer on their skin and in their hair, making faces, the chapped lips, fingertips resting on their temples, hands cupped over their chests, the vise-like grip of their legs, their breathing, being entwined in their sleep. How many children can a man sire (*be fruitful and multiply!*)? How many children can a woman bear? They had two and wanted only two. They could have afforded three or four, because his wife also worked, she did translations. But they wanted more out of life, a nice apartment, travel and college for the children, a better start. His wife never finished college. He never even made it through high school. She didn't throw that in his face. She worked, and they didn't have to pinch pennies. And when one of her translations was a success, she could be exuberant, not like him, he'd never been able to do that.

He watches the people getting on, the ones getting off, pale winter faces, tired movements, when are you really rested up for the day? Two more stops to go before he has to transfer. A day like this always begins with the same rhythm.

She watched him leave, just as she watches him leave every day, she waved, and he turned around at the lamp post near the corner, a gesture, a habit, perhaps only habit now, he turns around at the same place in summer and in winter. He left his coat unbuttoned, he always leaves his coat unbuttoned! and the wind got caught inside it. He looked as if he were about to fly away. Or perhaps not, it just seemed irresponsible to her, and she often warns him he's going to catch cold. But he doesn't listen when she says that, nor does he catch cold, not even when everyone else does, it's as if he wouldn't give her the pleasure of pampering him just once. She closed the window again and started her housework, the beds, the dishes, peeling potatoes, putting the laundry in to soak, her mind was already on the text she was translating, an American study about making a green zone around the perimeter of the city (the translation has to be delivered in ten days).

She always watched him leave in the morning, always waved, always waited for him in the evening. In the summer, he'd often picked a rose in the park, and later on, when they had the children, he'd bring something along for them, a bag of apples, a chocolate bar, just a little something. And after the children went to bed, they'd listen to records—gospels, which were becoming popular just then. Or, in the winter, they'd take the sled and head for the iced-over toboggan run in the park. They'd sat side by side in the funeral home, stood side by side at hospital beds, speechless, what's the matter, is it death? They'd paddled up to one another in the Baltic, the North Sea, Lake Ossiach and White Lake (Carinthia), caressed by the waves, side by side while treading water. Or they'd talked, talked and couldn't bring their daughter back with their talk, she'd taken off for some cellar in the city. They'd talked until they were empty, sat there at the table, waiting, and yet waiting no longer. And then he'd begun to do crossword puzzles, crossword puzzles everywhere, she found them filled out in every newspaper, a tributary of the Danube, of the Rhine, a French spa, a synonym for storm, a girl's name. She cleared the papers away every morning and bundled them up for Friday trash collection.

She hasn't turned the lights on yet, as she puts the paper in her typewriter. Eberhard should be at the office by now, fluorescent lights are easy on the eyes, he says. The sixty-watt bulb is enough for her.

He got off at the transfer station and went downstairs to the tunnel that connects the intersecting routes. And then he went down the next flight of stairs to the platform, where the trains stop every morning before or after intersecting with the other line (his). His train had come in on the right-hand side of the track. The other train was on the other side, doors open. The people who got off were just now reaching the bottommost steps. That was strange, since the other train had already left the station and he meets the people transferring from the opposite direction midway through the tunnel, where people hurrying from both directions are always bumping into one another. This time the approaching people won't make their train. He doesn't know why he stepped through one of the open doors into the no-smoking car, he hears the conductor call "All aboard!" and the doors close, he sees that all the seats are taken here as well. He can get off at the next stop. According to the schedule, his train will already have passed through there. He'll have to wait and be ten minutes late for work. He can offer some vague excuse as an apology, a headache or the alarm didn't go off, normally he is never late. But he doesn't get off when the train stops again. And because a seat is free now, he even sits down. It's nice to sit when you're still sleepy, nice to think that they'll be waiting for him at the office, that they'll miss him and won't forget him right away even though there's work to be done, Eberhard W.—Special Consultant, room 137, the messenger will leave the loan applications and the mail on his empty desk. It's nice to think that nobody knows where he's going (it's a wide, wide world! His boyhood longing to go on a polar expedition, he'd dreamed of crouching beside Amundsen in the gondola beneath the balloon, far below the jagged whiteness of the polar ice, or was it a dream at all?). It's nice to think that his wife, busy with her translation, has left the window long ago and has stopped waving, no longer clutches him with her worrying. And that's why he doesn't get out at the next stop, nor the one after that, he isn't counting anymore, no longer pays attention to the station names, senses that the train is slowly moving uphill, coming out of the tunnel. The lights go off. And it's daylight outside. Brown underbrush along the tracks, row houses he's not familiar with, coated with winter dinginess, shops with their lights still on inside, cars, a bus at a traffic light, people, dark and bundled up, a dog. The train comes into the next station, a glass waiting room. Nobody gets on. Most people have already gotten off, the last stop can't be far away. Beyond the glass waiting room: the street again on the other side of a fence, and now a narrow strip of green, light green, a manicured lawn. A few bits of paper (old newspapers) flutter up as the train passes. And then the last stop, the train going the other way on the other side of the platform. If he takes that one, he'll be scarcely an hour late getting to work. But he heads straight for the exit. It's windy when he comes out of the station, damp and cold, and it smells like dirt and chemicals. They're putting up factories all along the edge of town, pharmaceuticals, paint and varnish, synthetics, industries with no particular on-site needs, they don't even need railway connections, as long as the roads are in shape for trucks. He turns up his collar. Button your coat! he grins, because it has occurred to him yet again. He sticks his briefcase between his knees. It's hard to push the buttons through the buttonholes, and his fingers are numb. He picks up his briefcase again and shoves it under his arm, so he can put his hands in his pockets. He waits at the crosswalk in front of the newsstand, doesn't know whether he should go right or left, decides on the right, hesitates a moment longer after he's crossed the street and then marches off into the wind. His eyes are tearing and he's breathing heavily. Dozens of compact cars are parked on the unpaved lots in front of the new factories, red ones, green, canary yellow, blue, rust red, others painted with flowers and beetles. The chain link fences haven't started to rust, the buildings, set up out of pre-fab parts, are still white or pale yellow, a few splashes of mud on the walls. The changing shadows of the gray, withered bushes that still lie on the pile of trash left from last summer's construction. Along the road, which must have been a country road once, running over fields from village to village, the trees are still standing, oaks, they've defied the asphalt. Can they also defy the increasing commercial traffic in the new industrial district? Is their removal already included in development plans? He doesn't meet anyone he could ask, and he's not sure anyone could answer him. In the afternoon, people at work in the factories will get in their cars, start the engine and drive home. They don't care about the trees, at best they curse them when there's not enough room to pass another car. But what does he care about them? He couldn't care less what they make in the factories, pharmaceuticals or synthetics, paint or varnish. He marches on. They're going to pave the sidewalks next spring. Then it won't smell like dirt anymore, it will only smell like chemicals. Good that spring is still a long way off! Good that he came out here today! Good! Good! He catches himself whistling. He hasn't whistled in a long time.

When it's light enough to turn off the desk lamp, she takes a cigarette break. In the office, they'll be working now by daylight too. Can Eberhard also take a cigarette break? What is he doing? Does he see that it's clearing up, that it's going to be a nice day? A nice day, clear shadows, bright light, dust dancing up in lightbeams. Does Eberhard see that? His window faces south, she knows. What else does she know? Since the problem with their daughter, the crossword puzzles. And before that? Summer days, the children's birthdays, the way his strong, hairy hands would light the candles in the Chinese lanterns for the Halloween parade, the way they tied the children's shoes on Sundays before taking a walk, the way they clamped themselves to their parents' wrists like a pair of vises, back then when she wanted to get away, far, far away, when she didn't think she could stand it anymore in the cramped apartment where it always smelled of steaming laundry, of onions and cabbage, when she didn't want to believe that this was life. This! And she still felt the pain months later and had stayed, took care of the family, the children, the housekeeping, the smell of laundry, onions and cabbage. And had done a few commissioned translations, money for their savings account. After all, they wanted to get ahead, get a larger apartment—if that indeed is what life was. What else does she know?

That Eberhard shook his head when she went looking for their daughter in unfamiliar parts of town, at police stations. Let her be! Let her have her way! And he'd flipped through the newspapers looking for crossword puzzles. Even when they got the news.

And what else? She writes letters to their younger daughter, since all it takes is to put paper in the typewriter, he says; but before Christmas he goes shopping and packs a box "for the little one, so that she'll have a few good days," cuts the colorful wrapping paper carefully and nestles packet after packet in the large box lined with Excelsior, work for a Sunday, which he takes his time with, addressing tags, and before he closes the box, he lays a fir branch on top of the Excelsior. And what else? What else is there? He didn't say much about the war, he'd been lucky, he said, didn't have to shoot anybody, hadn't been wounded, no medals, nothing, even his captivity had been brief. And he'd found his father still in their apartment with all those schoolboy memories. The Hitler Youth uniform was all he'd thrown away, tossed in a pile of rubble. That was also in the past, the parade marches and maneuvers. He'd simply gone along with it, he says. And he'd taken the certificate proving he'd completed his training from the filing drawer where his father had saved it for him, and had run through the bombed-out city so he could report back to the savings and loan where he done his apprenticeship. He'd started to work in an unheatable, barely finished room on the first floor, which still had above it the four floors of a burned-out apartment house. She knows that, because she used to pick him up there at night when she didn't have class, which was also held in an unheatable, barely finished room not far from the partially destroyed university. She met him the second summer after the war on the dance floor of a beer garden. She noticed him as he tried to help someone up who obviously had an artificial leg and had fallen down.

And what else?

She's finished her cigarette. She has to concentrate on the translation, the greening of outlying urban zones, the deadline is almost here. She doesn't ask anymore what sense it makes to earn money, to save money. Back then it had been important, because they wanted to get married, did get married, wanted to have children, did have children, even though they wondered whether a future in which the atom bomb existed was any place for children. Because they didn't want to live alone anymore. Because they were young. Because two was company. Because—because. . .

She bends over the material she's translated so far, proofs, corrects, crosses out.

She must ask Eberhard tonight what he was thinking when they'd strolled hand in hand through the park on Sundays and watched the children, who were so thin and frail, but still played catch and laughed.

He feels hot. He's unbuttoned his coat again. His wife won't see it, this touching, burdensome worry, why should she care how he lives! A man of his age doesn't need a wife. Did he ever need her or she him? What was it anyway, their marriage? What is it? What will become of it? He feels his muscles, as he did when he was a boy. Growing pains, they called it back then, the pleasant, painful stretching sensation in your calves and thighs. You'll turn into a giant, my boy! His father's expectation, his own expectation, to grow, grow up, the untamed power in his arms, the shyness and the eagerness when he thought about girls, the dirty schoolboy jokes and the feeling of disgust about them, the dull fear during nighttime marches on weekends (*And when we're on the march, we're guided by a light*), knowing that war is of the masculine gender and that you shouldn't know it. Growing up, what is it anyway?

What was it? The smell of leather and sweat? He'd sung along, had squirmed with the others through the underbrush, through fields of rye, and over sprawling acres of turnips, and had gone to school on Monday with his hair combed wet and his hands scrubbed red. *You'll turn into a giant.* Soon he no longer believed that, in the face of numbers and customer accounts, in the face of the vault in the basement. He didn't think about it anymore once he was in the barracks. Leather and sweat and dirty jokes and the grease for oiling your rifle and the commands: *Left face! Right face! Halt! Forward march! March in place! Take cover!* War is of the masculine gender. Muscles and fatigue, night transports, drafty freight cars, their wheels clicking. He didn't talk about the war. He'd survived. Why does this occur to him, this particular thing! He hadn't told his wife how, in order to advance a section of the front, they'd been thrown ahead into a village, that they'd retaken it and how they'd found the people who had been hanged, men and women, how they'd buried them behind the barn, because they didn't want to get involved, didn't get involved.

He has to stop, take a deep breath. Isn't used to running anymore, nor the strenuous marching that makes your muscles ache, nor the wind that makes his eyes tear, that takes his breath away. He braces himself against a tree with his hand. The oak bark is hard, it hurts yet doesn't hurt, as if the hand weren't his. It's daylight, he thinks, day. They're going to pave the sidewalk next spring. How far off is that: spring? Their daughter was born in the spring. The trees were in bloom as they strolled about the community gardens with the baby carriage. He'd wanted to gather his wife and child up in his arms, never let them go, wanted all of it! that sort of a thing. Fathermotherchild. His wife had bent over the petals blown from the flowers. All of it. Fathermotherchild. He hadn't thought of that even once, nor had he helped her gather the petals. How long ago was that? How much longer? He hears the door slam shut. His wife is standing there, her shoulders drooping. I'm leaving now, their daughter said, no notice, no big scene, and I'm not coming back. His wife is standing there, her shoulders drooping. But that's all in the past. Even that. He wants to sit down, slips to the ground, rubs his hand raw. The smell of dirt. The smell of dirt and chemicals. Why do oaks have such hard bark? Freedom is soft. How did he come up with that? Everything is so hard here with you, their daughter had said, hard and matter-of-fact. Even your love is hard. But that was long before she'd left, when she cut off the hem of her pants and let her hair grow down to her hips and painted the red mark of Hindu women on her forehead, a passing whimsy. I don't want to become hard, don't want to turn into a giant, don't want to be someone who sings loudly on nighttime marches to drown out my fear, I don't, I don't. . . His palm is burning. He's gasping for air. I don't want to be hard, something stupid like that. He licks his sore palm, dogs lick their wounds, the sweet taste of blood, he wants to stand up, can't. Freedom is soft, the earth is soft before the frost; he's lying on his back, he knows that, because he can see the tree tops, the confusing array of branches and twigs against the restless, jagged white cloud cover (topsy-turvy world, way down, way up, polar ice, pack ice, he wants to yell: where are we? Where am I?). All you've ever known is order, their daughter said, from the time the alarm goes off in the morning until you go to bed at night. Why don't you say something? Why haven't you ever said anything? Those people who were hanged, did she want to know about them? Know about the horror for which no answer exists? For which he has found no answer?

His good hand reaches out, pulls up blades of grass, dry blades of grass.

He's gasping for air.

For the phone to ring between eleven and twelve is not unusual. A new assignment. Checking back. But she wasn't expecting that.

News very different from the time before, when they'd worried and waited for months without a word from their daughter: they've found Eberhard in the industrial park north of town. What on earth was he doing out there? The woman at the check-in desk in the hospital doesn't know either. Are you coming? You are his wife, aren't you?

Do what has to be done, take out the papers, insurance, hospitalization benefits, call a taxi. While putting on her coat she remembers how she waved to him and how she warned him not to be so foolish, day after day. Do what has to be done. St. Gertrude's. That's all the taxi driver needs to know. The meter is running. Crumpling your gloves in your hand. Curiously white hands. The bright, flat light. She clenches her teeth together to keep them from chattering. There was so much more she wanted to ask him. There was so much she wanted to tell him. That their life was good, maybe that. A stock phrase: good. Because after all, their youngest is content. Because the oldest perhaps wanted too much. Freedom, what is that? She'd also wanted to tell him that she liked walking beside him in the park, in the gardens, in the fields and on the beach when they were on vacation. And that at a company party once, she realized she knew nothing about him, he was one of many in a dark suit, back then silver gray ties were in fashion, he was standing amongst his colleagues, they'd sung, whistled, he was a good whistler, he tapped out the rhythm with his feet. She takes a twenty mark note from her wallet. Do what has to be done. Shut the car door, walk up the few steps to the hospital entrance, ask for the room number. She forgot the flowers, she realizes, when she sees the potted plants in the lobby. Nurses and aides in white jackets are waiting for the elevator, get in along with her. Do what has to be done. Check her hair in the elevator mirror, practice smiling, practice the first sentence: Eberhard, what on earth were you dreaming of! The second sentence, how will the second sentence go? The elevator stops. A long, waxed hallway (these waxers do a lot more than your mop at home!), count off the numbers up to his door, open it carefully, then the second, the inner door. A three-bed room, but two beds are empty. She tiptoes over to the bed at the window (just hold the gloves tightly, kid gloves, his Christmas present last year). He's strapped to the bed rails and hooked up to tubes, he looks pink. She can't think of the first sentence, the one that must be said, she notices that her hands are cold. She sees him breathe. His eyes are half-closed, he doesn't notice her, doesn't recognize her. She blows on her right hand, rubs it warm with her left, reaches out very slowly for his right hand, which looks as if it's been scratched inadvertently. Fingertip to fingertip. His mouth is half-open. He looks as if he's smiling. What could he be thinking? Is he thinking anything? She's not at all afraid anymore. She just wants to tell him—well, what, what? You, dear. That doesn't mean anything. Friends call each other dear. And if he opened his eyes? Eyes alone are nothing. Their daughter had pretty eyes, they always said. She had a pretty smile, is what they should have said, a smile for no one in particular or at least not for them, not for Mom and Dad. Fingertip to fingertip. The right hand, tightly bound, twitches. What does a hand say. You, dear. Me. Me. You. The news back then. They'd sat across from each other at the table. You, dear. Me. Me. You. You were a soldier. I was in school. You were no resistance fighter. And I never resisted, digging potatoes, collecting salvage, taking care of people who'd been bombed out, doing what had to be done, always. Our life too. Your life. My life. Their daughter had wanted something different. The happiness of being free. For her that was more than just a word. They learned about that after they got the news. The car had turned over, an old used car with bad tires. The leaflets had burned, a suitcase full of leaflets, black flakes of paper on the asphalt, a garbled account, freedom thrown away or not? A few young people came to offer their condolences, spoke of the impending peace in Vietnam, and that their daughter had worked for that. At the time they hadn't understood the young people. And now? Now?

Fingertip to fingertip. Only the soft humming of the machine. She'll have to ask if they are helping him breathe, later, when the nurse comes. And how the machine works. And how long it can keep on doing it. She whispers his name, she doesn't know if he hears it. She could call out loud, but that's not how it's done, and she doesn't know if he would hear her. The flat November light stands in the room, no dancing particles of dust. The sentence in her translation occurs to her, the one she'd interrupted: kitchen gardens grow wild so quickly, that—and the deadline she has to meet. And she's ashamed about it.

He wants to tell her something. He knows that she'd listen. But he can't talk. He draws his free left hand back from hers, senses the distance, the tension of distance. Trees are pretty in November, occurs to him, trees are clear against the jagged whiteness. And that that's no news. Not that. And besides, he can't talk. He raises his head, straining upward from the back of his neck. He waves, motioning for her to go, she shouldn't wait. Waves with his free left hand at the tension of distance. Knows that that's no news. Not even that.

THREE POEMS

ALLEN GROSSMAN

THE SONG OF THE LORD

There is a table bountifully spread.

In the full sunlight when there is no cloud
And under cloudy skies,
And when there are no stars and when the stars
Distill the time,

the table stands in a field.
It is late morning and the service shines.
The guests have wandered from the company.
The Lord is alone.

It is good to hear
The voice of the Lord at rest in his solitude.

The guests have wandered from the table set,

But they hear the voice of the Lord at rest:

The song of the Lord in solitude goes up,
Ten times enfolded, blue, and saturate
With law to the heavens at noon of gaze,

And down among the graves and the darker animals.
The song of the Lord indicates the dust
Of the roadway, the random hammer of the sea,
The riddled vase of mind and mind's dependencies

And pain lost otherwise and lost in this.

The voice of the Lord opens the gates of day.
Air streams through our eyes and brushes the pupils

Streams through our eyes and this is how we see.

NOVEMBER, OR JEALOUSY

1
My sister, my lover,

what are these tears?
There is a general sadness in the cold,
November rain. Everything is strange, as
In itself it is
Bound to its own or another's interest,
But not to me. The look of the light is turned.
Something makes me ignorant of my life,
And all my words provisional. . . .

* * *

Night after night (all of the nights) my sister
Sleeps with her husband,
And only for certain moments of the day
Is she mine; and so it is with all things—
Faithless, averted earth. And within me
My mind, in the sexual power of another,
Is drawn down by the gravity of his claim.
I shall never be the only lover of
My sister:

always before my eyes her body
Is naked, as I have known it, on a bed;
And another lover—I recognize—opens her
Legs with his knee, and her sex with his fingers
Which know what they can have. He enters her,
And she is covered from my sight except
A caressing hand along his back, and the gleam
Of a look absorbed in a life that does
Not know me. . . .

It is raining. She has taken in his seed.
What are they doing now in the one bed?
I must simplify my thought—or die.
Surely the intercourse of brother and sister
Is simple as rain falling in water
Is simple utterly.

2

My sister, my lover,

We have but one body
Which is not ours, witness of unknown histories—
Like a square tower with an iron door
In a field,
That a man and woman come upon
Walking together in the November rain
And are astonished—and look at one another,
For the first time seeing the strangeness. . .
"Who made it?" they ask. "How did it come here?"
"What has befallen?"

* * *

And there is no thought so patient, nor look
So long, nor moment of attentiveness forested
So deep in quietness that the loved body
Is really found asleep in its true form;
Or the oak tree of stature startled
From perpetual reverie of her other

Lover, the sun; or the stars of night touched
At the punctual moment of their burning. . . .

And so I look out in tears from the square tower,
Seeing a man and woman find the path
Once more, after their brief astonishment—
And disappear out of the ruined empire
Of November's field.

Then I look again
And see a crowd of men and women naked
In the smoky rain burning the plague garments
Of memory.

And for the last time look
And see night rising,
And on the iron door the Winter shuts
A great lock, and sets his ignorant seal. . .

Do not pity me.

3
My sister, my lover,

nothing is clean
Against this cold.
In the night air, a vast circling disturbance:
The man and woman, her cries and his dark howling,
Fuck on the unmade bed of Winter wind,
The snow coming on.
And I hear the parent tongues of all my uttering,
Her voice caressing him
(Why does she not cover herself?) and also
The other voice of the dark man which penetrates
Her body and is effective,

And weep because the poem is never true.

* * *

No man or woman can utter the true
Poem of a whole life,
Or of a single day, or of one moment
Of the common day;
Yet they walk on, nonetheless, over the rainy,
Promiscuous earth, and do not speak more
Of the unforgettable sentiment—
Of the square tower, or of the dark man
Who will come between them in the end.

And this wild November field, the great world—
Wintering wasps of it, and the lodged grasses,
The rain-worn faces of old nests, clear
Traces of burning, and dark shadow over
Of the cold storm—
Is the only secret of every soul
That lives
And a song to each alone. And consoles
The dead such as are in pain, and rejoices
The dead such as are in joy, and draws on
The dead that have not finished. . .

"It is simple, my brother, as falls this
Voice into your heart
Where only my name is, as water into
Water after rain,
Water dropping, shining, disappearing
Into water."

QUIES, OR REST

A woman goes from room to room. She extinguishes
One light in each room. Darkness follows her
And in the last room she is overtaken.
Then, she mounts the dark stair confidently
And enters the room she sleeps in, and lies
Down in the dark, where a man in the dark wakes
A little and covers her with his arm.

VARIATIONS ON A HELIOTROPE OF RAINER MARIA RILKE

HOWARD STERN

1 PERSIAN HELIOTROPE

For your friend, Praise of the Rose might seem too bold:
Take the embroidered heliotrope, the plant
that urgently whispers; overchant
the Nightingale, who stridently extolled

her name in every public square she graced
and never knew her. For behold, and mark:
Like sentences that huddle in the dark
their honeyed words, all separateness erased;
the vowels' violet and wakeful red
perfuming quiet canopy and bed—:

so stars that are distinct will close in muster
over the quilted leaves to form a cluster;
blending silence, cinnamon, and delight
to deliquescence, essence of the night.

2 INDO-EUROPEAN HELIOTROPOLOGY

It seems quite likely that hyperbole
would overdo it. Wiser to understate
her virtues—when you find one, imitate
a plant that mumbles to itself. Then she

can't be standoffish: she'll ask you to date her.
Whisper sweet uncommonplaces in
her perfumed ear. When you've induced her (later)
up to hear your etchings, spike her gin
with several drops of tasteless synaesthesia.
Inhibitions? Gone with the mind. Amnesia.

So words resolve their prudishly phonemic
differences, blend endings, mix morphemic
melodies into a sillabub
of syllables: the sweet dessert of love.

3 VITO "DA BOID" USIGNOLO TO HIS NEPHEW VITO "DA LIDDLE BOID" ELIOTROPIO

Swaddyatink? A liddle pome in French
is gonna drive a goil like Rosie bonkuz?
Vnella shoibut? Poifume? Yeah, in Yonkuz
yuz cd probbly knock ya sweetie off da bench

wid candy pomes. Bud in da cidy, boidie,
ya hafta do it big. Foist fancy speeches,
den a stringa alldiffrun poils—zwat teaches
Rose dat ya mean business. Hoidy-toidy
Easside dolls wid doormen frunna deir homes,
dey don pud out fa poifume a fa pomes.

Dimportun tings ta neva ged cunfoosed.
Keep evenins fa da fambly, nyill ged used
ta nookyin in da sunlight. Don lose ya head.
Don call da missuz Rose. Don ead in bed.

4 MADAME NATASHA SPECULATES INTO THE RECENT FUTURE

Ah! Iss cahmink a nyew men eento you life.
Weet rosess? Nyet, impwossible. Ahnahder
fwonny plent. Iss tcheapsket? Sahmtink bwahder
me about mens vwoice. Xeess nozzy wife*

xeff earss een tyelescopp? Iss xwhy men mahmble?
Nyet, impwossible. Iss only beshful.
Poyet. Xwhere iss cahmink from? From Neshville?
Speak weet xeavy eccent. Mahmble-tchahmble:
"Tseena Mohnva Neelee Sespa Reelee"—
Iss vwoodoo wedding coorse? Iss bed Swaxili?

Iss maybe—nyet, impwossible. Natasha
start to smyellink music meekst weet kasha.
Poyet invyent sweet tsimbalom off pession.
Xahndred bahcks. Nyekst week ahnahder syession.

* *X* as in Russian (kh).

5 A DAY IN THE LIFE OF MAX LÖWENPREIS, FLORIST AND WAG

Hallo. Hier Maxens flauer schopp. Wie heff
a speschl nau on teiger lillies bei se
dossen. *Wie belieben?* Schutt bie *leise?**
Longstem roses mehby. Leik dschireff

im wachs museum, seldom giff a *Mucks.*
Na, heliotrop is lausy. *Zwanzig* dollars,
un so *meschugge* leik an ajatollers
bohring spietsches. Dschost a teiny *Jux.*
Heff no eidieja. Watt em ei, a goht?
Ei neffer iet semm. (*Mensch, ein Vollidiot!*)

* To be pronounced as though in German: Wie belieben: How's that again?; leise: soft, quiet; Mucks: peep (of protest); Jux: joke.

Ei tell ju watt ju du. Ju mehk a foto
off reckord off Fritz Kreisler *spiel*ing Moto
Perpetuo off Bambl-bie und send
se foto wis samm bonbons tu *dein* frend.

6 BALBULUS BALBULORUM DICIT CARMEN

Rosa sicut Persica puellae
clamat os. Quid dixi? Sicut flos
in campo. Sed hoc melius: o formos-
a! duo dentes tui sunt gemellae

columbarum. Peius est. Amarum
sicut vinum sentio puellae
claros pedes. Quid? Quasi gemellae
redolent lunae, rident capellarum
ubera. Tuarum? Suavis Musa!
mihi vero facta es Medusa.

Sed iubes me dolorem renovare.—
Saporem ineffabilem spectare
me delectat vocis tuae. Mene
fugis? Oculos avertis? Bene.

7 A DISSERTATION ON THE MARQUIS DE SADE, SO NOW I'M EDITORIAL ASSISTANT IN CHARGE OF . . .

Thank you ever so much for your submitting
Horticultured Verse. The editors judge it
worthy of publication, but our budget
doesn't agree. Right now we're not committing

funds to poets who aren't *already* dead.
Would you consider advice? Grind up a ballad
or sonnet from your book to garnish a salad
of Persian melon and passion fruit. In bed,

slurp ice cream with it. Blend a vanillanelle
or incestina. Why not? What the hell!

There isn't much work for poets in the city,
but everyone eats, almost. You're sitting pretty
with gourmet verse or light digestible prose.
(Signed) Florence Nightingale, for Harpy & Rose.

8 FINALE: A HUNDRED SMACKERS, AND ALL HE EVER SAYS IS "TELL ME ABOUT IT"

The creep I dated last was a musician.
Punk rock outfit called the Night-in-Jails.
Arena's crammed with people, this loudmouth wails:
"O Rosie let me be yer electrician—

I'm Eveready forya." What's the good?
I'm tired of playing a Kewpie on the shelf.
I'll give up men and learn to love myself,
as any self-respecting woman should.
This guy I met in Writers' Workshop though,
he's sort of cute, he's sort of . . . I don't know . . .

refined. His love songs have an almost quichey
sound, he drones them like a maharishi.
But maybe I'll invite him home to tea.
And one thing is for sure, he's sweet on me.

A SENSE OF HUMOR

ALAN M. BROWN

She suspects that people don't trust the post office during the holiday season so she tries to stay off the telephone, waits for friends to call in their invitations to Christmas parties.

At the office, her co-workers complain loudly about all the parties they have to go to, and when Darlene asks Miriam, the Jewish girl in the cubicle next to hers, if she'd like to come by and help trim her tree, Miriam says, "I'd love to, Darlene, I would really love to. But, can you believe it, I don't have one free night in the next two weeks. You know how it is around Christmas."

Darlene sympathizes; yes, she knows how it is, and then she suggests a Sunday morning tree-trimming, but Miriam has a brunch date.

On Friday night, Darlene goes out with a man she has known for almost two years. Sometimes James does not call her for months at a time, but she never has the nerve to bring this to his attention. They eat dinner at a small Chinese restaurant near Golden Gate Park, and then they just drive around. This is something James really likes to do: just drive around. James is a real estate agent and every time he sells a house he trades in his car for a newer and flashier model. His latest one is all silver and chrome and looks a little like one of those two-man rocket ships from *Star Wars*, Darlene thinks. Inside, red digital numbers blink on the dashboard like a computer console.

They pass a small repertory theater house in Darlene's neighborhood and she says, on impulse, "Let's go to the theater." She doesn't even know what is playing.

"Now?" James slows the car a bit and looks at her.

"Yes, don't you want to go to a play?" she says.

"You mean, right now?"

"Yes." Darlene is surprised at her own decisiveness.

"Not right this minute," James says.

"Why not?" she asks.

"Do you really want to go to a play right now?" James wants to know. James is tall and very imposing; his head touches the roof of his new little rocket ship.

"I guess not." Darlene looks at her watch. "I guess we couldn't just walk right in off the street and expect to see a play, anyhow."

When James takes her home, he doesn't ask to spend the night, and she doesn't invite him inside. He doesn't even wait until she unlocks her front door before he guns the engine and blasts off down the street.

Darlene assesses herself in the full-length mirror behind her bedroom door this Saturday morning, five days before Christmas. She knows that she is pretty, knows this for a fact, has been told it enough times in her life to believe it. She is tall, but not too tall to scare off men, and her figure is nice. Not special, but nice. Her eyes—blue—and her hair—almost black—are her best features, and she takes especially good care of her hair, washing it nightly, brushing it one hundred strokes on each side before going to bed.

Darlene is pretty sure that she has a good personality. When she was growing up, her mother had this to say of her and her sister: "Darlene has the looks and Penelope has the personality." Darlene always secretly felt that her mother just said that to make Penny feel better. Penny had a bad complexion all through high school and spent her Friday and Saturday nights babysitting for neighbors.

The phone finally does ring on Saturday afternoon, late, and Darlene waits three rings before she will pick it up. It is her friend, Richard, and he wants her to meet him for coffee. Richard lives four blocks away with his lover, Roger. They own a frame shop on Union Street and are always giving Darlene beautiful wood frames that have only very small cracks in them, cracks you can't really see unless you are looking for them. Richard is from Darlene's hometown, outside of Chicago; they have been friends since high school.

On her way to the cafe, Darlene walks down Castro Street. She is wearing her suede jacket and a new maroon scarf that accentuates her eyes. There are Christmas displays in all of the store windows and there is a giant Christmas tree, maybe twenty feet high or more, in the Hibernia Bank Plaza. The tree is decorated with very ugly, white wreaths that are made of some furry material Darlene can't identify. When she is directly in front of the tree, she stops. Near the bottom, someone has hung a copy of the Beatles' "Sgt. Pepper's Lonely Hearts Club Band." The record jacket is open to the photo on the inside of the four Beatles. They are wearing band uniforms and the background is bright yellow. The album is attached to the green branches by four red ribbons which are threaded through small holes punched in the corners of the cover. This makes Darlene feel bad for two reasons:

First, because she forgot to observe the silence in memory of John Lennon's death that past Sunday. Instead, she spent the morning on the telephone, chatting away about nothing in particular to her sister in Los Angeles. Later, when she watched the six o'clock news and saw hundreds of thousands of people all over the world who were able to get it together to keep quiet for only ten minutes, she felt foolish.

The album cover on the Christmas tree also makes her feel bad because it reminds her of how old she is. Very few things make Darlene feel old; she is, after all, only thirty-two. But John Lennon's death does. She remembers when she was fifteen and she went out and had her hair cut like Jean Shrimpton's, with long bangs in front, and then went into town with a girlfriend on a Saturday afternoon and spent her savings on a black leather hat just like the one John wore. Most of her friends liked Paul because he was so pretty, but she loved John and even carried a book of his poetry with her all through her sophomore year in high school. Some of the poems she could recite from memory.

Richard is already seated at a table against the wall when Darlene arrives at the cafe, but he has waited to order. They both order cappucino, and, when the waiter returns with their cups, two pieces of chocolate layer cake. There is a glass display case on the other side of the narrow room, with four rows of cakes, pies, and pastries that revolve, lit dramatically from underneath. After they order the chocolate cake, Richard goes and stands by the case, looking at the desserts, changing his mind again and again, until Darlene becomes impatient and makes him sit down.

"What are you getting me for Christmas?" Richard wants to know. Richard is very handsome. His hair is light brown and wavy. He has small, thin lips and nice rosy cheeks like apples. Darlene sometimes wants to pinch his cheeks, but she restrains herself. Darlene used to dream about sleeping with Richard, and once, when they were at a party and were both very drunk on tequila, she told him so. He didn't look as surprised as she thought he should.

"I don't know what I'm getting you," Darlene says. "And even if I did, I wouldn't tell you. You'll just have to wait and see."

"Want to know what I'm getting you?" Richard is teasing her, she can tell by the way he smiles, without showing his teeth.

"What?" Darlene sprinkles chocolate powder from a shaker into her cup.

"Refrigerator magnets," Richard says. "Little, enameled refrigerator magnets shaped like tiny animals. Giraffes. Rhinos. Camels. Tiny, enameled camels. I got them on Market Street."

"Wonderful," Darlene says. "That's just what I need, actually. My notes keep falling off the refrigerator door. I write messages to myself and then they keep falling on the floor and then I forget to do the things the notes were supposed to remind me to do."

"That's not really what I'm getting you," Richard says. He looks hurt.

"I know that, Richard. Don't you think that I know that?"

He brightens instantly. "But I did really buy them on Market Street. They're hideous. I'm going to give them to everyone I don't like."

"If you don't like some people, why are you giving them gifts?" Darlene wants to know.

"Christmas spirit," Richard answers her.

Darlene goes back to Richard's apartment with him to help wrap his presents. Roger is down at their frame shop, but Albie, Roger's brother, is there. Albie is a juggler, and he works at Pier 39. All of his friends are clowns and acrobats. Once, at a party Richard and Roger gave, Darlene found herself talking to a man who made his living diving off of a fifty-foot platform into a small pool of water. At that same party, which was a birthday party for one of Roger's friends, there was a big box in the middle of the living room wrapped with yards of pink ribbon. When it was time for the birthday cake, a clown burst out of the box and threw a pie in the face of the guest of honor. Everyone applauded.

It is Albie's day off and now he is in the kitchen juggling two long knives and a rolling pin. He is happy to see Darlene but she won't talk to him while he is practicing because it makes her nervous. When he is finished, he comes into Richard's bedroom where they are wrapping gifts. Darlene is running one blade of a scissor along a taut ribbon to make it curl, then she tapes it to the top of a Macy's box.

"What are you doing for Christmas, Darlene?" Albie wants to know. He stands in the doorway balanced on one foot, juggling four oranges.

"I haven't decided yet," Darlene says. "I have a few invitations and I have to decide which one to accept." This is a lie, but she doesn't want to admit to him that she has nothing to do. Darlene thinks that Albie, with his smooth skin and long, curly hair, is very good-looking, but he is only twenty-seven years old so she is always careful not to let on. When they first met, he asked her out on dates twice, and both times she reluctantly refused. Darlene's mother says that dating a younger man is a sign of immaturity.

"Well, I'm having a Christmas dinner. You could add my invitation to your list," Albie offers. "You could come to my place." Albie lives alone in a very small, one-room apartment in the Mission, which is why he spends so much time at Roger and Richard's place.

"Thank you, Albie," Darlene says. "But I don't think so."

"You should come," Richard says. "We're going. You should come with us."

"I'll let you sit at the head of the table," Albie says.

"Well," says Darlene. "I'll see."

Albie disappears into the hall for a minute and returns dragging a large, theatrical trunk along the floor.

"What's in the suitcase?" Darlene asks.

"Clown stuff," he says, laying the trunk down against the wall.

"Stuff?" she says.

"Costumes," he says. "I'm trying out new costumes for my act.

Here." Albie pulls Darlene to her feet and begins to dance her around the room. She feels like a dead weight. She can't get her feet moving, and she is embarrassed in front of Richard.

"Be a clown," Albie sings. "Everybody loves a clown."

And before she can stop him, Albie is helping her into a bright harlequin's costume with a ridiculously frilly collar and a floppy top hat. He pulls a bulbous nose down over her head, attached to an elastic band. He whirls her around and around while Richard applauds and laughs, then stops her suddenly in front of the mirror. Richard fakes a drum roll with his hands on the floor.

"Presenting," Albie the ringmaster shouts, "presenting Madame Darlene, Queen of the Clowns. Ta da."

"Brava, brava," Richard yells. "Send in the clowns. Send in the clowns."

Darlene tries to laugh, but, in truth, she is horrified by her own reflection: the elastic band pushing her hair up into a grotesque shape; the big, red nose distorting her face. Her body is a comic sack of potatoes, and she is too humiliated to look at Albie or Richard, so she runs from the room.

"Hey," Albie whispers, knocking gently on the bathroom door. "Hey, I'm sorry. Really I am."

Darlene has ripped the clown's clothes from her body, is sitting on the toilet seat combing her hair back into place. "Leave me alone," she says. "You were making fun of me."

"No," he whispers. "No fun. I thought you looked beautiful." He waits, but she doesn't answer. "I thought you were the prettiest clown I'd ever seen."

Darlene takes the bus home from Richard's apartment. It is only four blocks, but it is all uphill and it is easier than walking. There is heavy traffic on Castro Street, holiday traffic, and the bus driver must do some fancy maneuvering to get the bus across the intersection at Market Street. Darlene is sitting right up front and when an old man gets off on the next corner he pats the driver on the shoulder and says, "You're an artist."

"I try to be," the driver says as the old man carefully steps down to the sidewalk.

Darlene's mother calls that night to ask Darlene what she is doing for Christmas. It is snowing in the Midwest and Darlene's mother opens her window and holds the receiver out so that Darlene can hear the snow. She cannot hear the snow but she can hear the sound of tires spinning on the icy streets.

Then Darlene's mother holds the receiver up to Sparky, so that Darlene can say hello to their cat. Sparky is fourteen years old. When Darlene first brought Sparky home, when he was just a six-week-old kitten, Darlene's mother refused to touch him, and she would only pick him up with a dish rag. Now, Darlene's mother gives Sparky bowls of warm milk that she heats in a saucepan over the stove. Every night, she opens three cans of cat food, three different flavors, and puts them on the kitchen floor for Sparky to choose from. Some nights, he doesn't choose any of them.

"Say hello to Darlene, baby," Darlene's mother says to the cat, trying to make him purr. "Say hello like a good little kitty cat."

Her mother does not mention the fact that it is Saturday night and her daughter does not have a date, although there once was a time when she would have. She gave up when Darlene turned thirty. Darlene's mother always wanted big weddings for her two daughters, and when Darlene turned thirty, she had this to say on that subject: "Of course, at your age, a big wedding is out of the question. At your age, it's best to do it as quickly and quietly as possible."

Darlene knows that her mother means well, and mostly, she leaves her alone. Once, though, her mother told her that her main problem was that she, Darlene, lacked a sense of humor. "You take yourself too seriously," she said. "You have to laugh more. You have to laugh at yourself."

"But I do," Darlene said. "I laugh a lot. All the time."

Darlene's sister disappointed their mother by eloping, although the whole family was very pleased with her selection of a husband. "She did very well for herself, all things considered," Darlene's mother said to her, meaning, of course, by "all things considered," Penny's looks. Penny's husband is a plastic surgeon and many of his patients are movie stars. Penny sometimes fills in for his receptionist and once, when Darlene was visiting Los Angeles, her sister took her down to the office in Century Plaza and Darlene sat with her behind the desk for the entire afternoon. She saw a few famous faces pass through her brother-in-law's office door, including one that she had recently seen praised for her youth and natural beauty on a national talk show.

On Sunday morning, Darlene wakes up to a beautiful day. The sky is clear and when she opens up the window next to her bed, the breeze is warm and fresh as if it were spring instead of the weekend before Christmas. Sometimes the seasons get mixed up in California, she thinks as she looks down at the flowering peach tree in the front yard. The tree is just beginning to turn and the ground is covered with yellow and red leaves. It is autumn in Darlene's front yard.

After her shower, Darlene opens up all of the windows in her apartment, and she stands in front of the bathroom mirror. It is steamed up but she clears a circle on the glass with the palm of her hand and she considers her hair. She experiments. She grabs hold of a big pile of hair with both hands and pushes it up on top of her head. She turns this way and that, looks critically at her profile. She arranges her hair in a variety of ways around her head, and, as she does this, she wrinkles her forehead, unconsciously, in an expression of concentration.

It is too nice a day to do nothing, Darlene thinks, and she decides to take a bus down to North Beach and to walk to Pier 39. She thinks that Albie will be working and that it would be a nice day to watch him juggle.

Darlene walks towards the back of the bus, but there is a middle-aged couple arguing in the last seat. The man says something to the woman, puts his face right up to hers, speaks right into her face. The woman draws back from him and shouts, "Don't you 'Merry Christmas' me!" Darlene turns around and goes back up front to sit near the driver.

Darlene window shops along Columbus Avenue, and near Washington Square, she runs into J.J. and Andy. J.J. is in Darlene's Wednesday night jazz exercise class, and twice she has had Darlene over for dinner after class, although Darlene has never reciprocated. Andy is the man she lives with. J.J. and Andy are both very short and dark, and today they are wearing matching red sweaters with green scarves. Darlene thinks that they look like Christmas tree ornaments.

J.J. always wears a gold nose ring, and once, she came to jazz exercise class with a thin gold chain connecting that to an earring. Although she knew it made no sense, Darlene was afraid that every time J.J. turned her head the chain would rip the ring out of her nose.

"Wait until you see Andy's new trick," J.J. says to Darlene as the three of them stand on the sidewalk absorbing the morning sunlight.

"Come on, Andy," she says to the little bearded man. "Give Darlene a dog."

"A what?" Darlene says. "What dog?" She does not understand.

"You'll see," says J.J., and she giggles.

Andy walks up to Darlene, leans right into her body and begins, like a dog, sniffing loudly up and down the side of her face, his thick nose poking into the skin of her cheek, his beard scratching her neck. Before she can push him away, Andy is licking her face, his wet tongue darting in and out of her ear, down under her chin, to the collar of her coat.

"Arf," says Andy, when he is done, and he lifts his little hands up like a puppy begging for a biscuit, paws at the air.

"Isn't he just wonderful?" J.J. wants to know. She squeezes Andy around the waist, kisses him on his forehead.

"Merry Christmas," Darlene says, and begins walking towards Fisherman's Wharf.

"Come by for some eggnog," J.J. says, but Darlene does not turn around.

Albie is working with three other men today, and they are surrounded by a large crowd when Darlene reaches Pier 39. On the edge of this crowd is a man dressed as a tomato, with red tights and a little green bonnet, handing out flyers for a new vegetarian restaurant on the Pier. Darlene works her way up to the front as the four men begin tossing striped beach balls and a pile of dinner plates back and forth. Albie and another man are riding unicycles as they juggle.

"Hey, Darlene," Albie yells when he spots her, and, between dinner plates, he waves. "Merry Christmas, love of my life."

Darlene is embarrassed as everyone turns and looks at her. Later, during his break, Albie takes her for lunch to a restaurant where the placemats are maps of San Francisco and everything on the menu is named after a tourist attraction. Darlene orders a Twin Peaks Burger and a Mission Milkshake. Albie is charming and when his dessert comes, he balances a spoon on his nose for the waitress.

"So," he says as they walk back across the crowded pier. Everyone is staring at them because Albie is dressed in big clown's shoes and baggy pants with fire engine-red suspenders.

"So what?" Darlene wants to know.

"So, now that we had lunch together, you're going to have to come to my place for Christmas dinner." Albie reaches behind Darlene's ear and pulls out a silver dollar.

"I can't," Darlene says, and as soon as she says it she wishes she could take it back. But she won't back down. "I would really like to, but I already told these people that I would come to their house. They're expecting me."

"Which people?" Albie asks.

"These people," Darlene says. "You don't know them. Just some people from work."

"Phooey," Albie says, and, right there in the middle of the pier, he stands on his head. "I'm holding my breath till I turn blue unless you say 'Yes.' "

"Look," says Darlene, who is thinking that Albie looks cute even upside-down. "Look, why don't you and Roger and Richard come by at night, after your dinner? Mine's in the afternoon; I'll be back by then and you can come for drinks."

"Drinks?" Albie says.

"Eggnog," says Darlene. "O.K.? Do you like eggnog?"

"Drinks. Christmas night." Albie repeats as if he is memorizing a list. "See you then," he says, and, pushing himself up, he walks away on his hands. Every few steps, he balances on one arm and waves back at Darlene until he is lost in the crowd and she can only see the bottoms of his big clown shoes sticking up over the heads of the Christmas shoppers.

Darlene buys a small Christmas tree and on Christmas day, she decorates it as she watches holiday specials on television. As Bing Crosby, Danny Kaye, Vera Ellen and Rosemary Clooney link arms and sing "White Christmas," she strings popcorn and cranberries. As three animated Wise Men come upon a cartoon Baby Jesus, she cuts five-pointed stars out of aluminum foil and hangs them from the tiny branches with hairpins. The telephone rings twice but she does not answer it, and when she walks past her window, she ducks down just in case. She bakes Christmas cookies and dusts them with powdered sugar. She makes the eggnog, following the recipe on the back of the rum bottle, and then she refrigerates it while she showers, washes and dries her hair. By six, Darlene is dressed in a new kelly-green turtleneck sweater and slacks, and she is pleased by her reflection in the bathroom mirror. She turns off the television and puts soft music on the record player, turns off the big lamp in her living room and turns on the blinking Christmas tree lights.

By seven, Darlene is absolutely starving. She had no Christmas dinner. She puts cheese and crackers out on a tray, takes the saran wrap off of the plate of Christmas cookies, then pours herself a great big glass of eggnog. She drinks it quickly and she pours herself another glass, and then another, as she arranges the wine glasses and cocktail napkins on her coffee table, puts the presents she bought for her friends under the tree.

At eight o'clock, the telephone rings, and Darlene answers it, but it is her mother and father calling to wish her a Merry Christmas. This cheers Darlene considerably, and, after they hang up, she calls her sister and brother-in-law in Los Angeles to wish them the same. Darlene and her sister talk for the longest time and Darlene carries both the telephone and her glass of eggnog into the bathroom with her, stares at herself in the bathroom mirror. Darlene is overflowing with holiday cheer, and, as she talks, she takes her brightest lipstick and draws a big clown's smile around her mouth. She powders her face white and dots her nose and cheeks with red freckles. When she is done talking to her sister, Darlene rummages through her closet until she finds: a baggy, white shirt that had belonged to her father; a floppy, wide-brimmed hat that she bought once on a vacation in Hawaii and never wore again.

At nine o'clock, the doorbell rings. It is Richard and Roger and Albie. And they stand on Darlene's doorstep for a long time before they finally decide that she must still be out to dinner and they leave. But Darlene is not out. And if Richard had only hoisted Roger up onto his shoulders, and if Albie had only climbed on top of Roger and stood on the tips of his toes to peek, like an acrobatic burgler, into her living room window, he would have seen Madame Darlene, Queen of the Clowns, curled up and asleep under her tiny tree, under a twinkling sky of aluminum foil stars.

FIVE POEMS

JOYCE CAROL OATES

WINTER CEMETERY

Abruptly, here, adrift in snow.
Grave yielding to grave.
The chiselled words a plane of ice,
the old marriages erased.
Who can tell one of us from another?—
or remember the old fierce quarrels?
I am here! I am no other!
Death isn't a legal matter now,
a test of boundaries,
or flesh,
here, adrift in snow.

An angel's pocked hand lifts in warning.
The head is encased in white,
the angry eyes are crusted over.
Why do we laugh suddenly?—
our mirth surprising us in
tiny puffs of steam?
This is the Catechism's final reply—
here, adrift.

WINTER SOLSTICE

The year gone in hillocks of white,
white seas, sandbars, tides
frozen in white—
that glassy interior.
The storm has lost its motion
and is now purely form.

This is the pitiless North we deserve,
the year gone in mouthfuls,
tiny bones,
pebbles.
This is true finitude:
the soul speaking in a perfect O.

FOLLIES OF WINTER

—Here I am, I said,
I've arrived at last—
driving day and night
and unsleeping—
I have been so good!—
and they stared at me:
Who are you? And why?

* * *

No one has walked across this field before

But those footsteps must be ours

Have we doubled back on ourselves

We crossed through the cemetery,
there was that creek—

—these barbed wire fences—

We can't be lost: the sun is a guide

Why can't we see the road from here

Is that a silo in the distance

Those must be our footsteps

We must have doubled back

But we've never been here before

* * *

Why did he work so hard,
if only to die?—
so my friend's widow asked me
as if I were to blame.
She was too angry to weep,
she'd had enough of that.
Why did he work so hard,
she accused.

A question posed
by every mirror in the arcade.

THE EVE OF YOUR DEATH

Today, a Sunday.
Consider motion.
Snow-bright horizontals gridding verticals,
country roads intersecting country roads,
in motion,
today,
the unacknowledged eve of your death.

The contours of the map are misshapen by snow,
snowfields yield to snowfields,
there is a certain levity to motion
if one doesn't ever stop.
And all is held in calm restraint by horizontals grid-
ding verticals.

It is always, in theory,
the eve of a death: but we are distracted
at once by ice-rippled winter streams
and clouds wispy as memory drifting across—which sky?
(This sky's beauty is porcelain,
our words harden to silence.)

In theory it is always *the eve of,*
the morning of, the final afternoon of,
as, in motion, morning shades to dusk
and strangers' children are observed sledding on a distant hill
in rhythm with your faltering breath.

Today, a Sunday.
Consider motion.
The soulless plenitude of snowy fields,
the fancied mourning of leafless trees,
textures the mere eye cannot gauge.
A giddy certainty to motion,
momentum experienced as fate.
Somewhere else a telephone is ringing.
We drive the country roads speeding and slowing,
skidding on snowy curves,
adrift,
in motion,
horizontals gridding verticals,
asphalt gridding macadam.
Perpetual motion.

WINTER NOONTIDE

And the sun is ablaze,
again gay as a pinwheel.
Drunk with light.

And we too are drunk.
Tottering on ice,

steamy breaths together,
gloved hands in gloved hands,
eager to forgive.

The sun *is* a child's pinwheel,
altogether innocent.
The sky is that hard enamel blue
that forgets so much.

THREE POEMS

HAYDEN CARRUTH

THE SOCIOLOGY OF TOYOTAS AND JADE CHRYSANTHEMUMS

Listen here, sistren and brethren, I am goddamn tired of hearing you tell me how them poor folk, especially black, have always got a Cadillac parked in the front yard, along with the flux of faded plastic and tin. I just blew fourteen thou, which make no mistake is the bankroll, on a Toyota Celica. "The poor man's sports car," the salesman said, which is the truth. (I'll write about the wrongs done to car salesmen another time.) She do look mighty good there in my front yard, too, all shiny red and sleek as a seal. It means a lot to me, like something near or almost near what I've always wanted, and it reminds me of the Emperor Tlu whose twenty-first wife asked him what he wanted for his birthday, and he being a modest man said the simplest thing he could think of offhand, a jade chrysanthemum, and thirty years later he got it, because you see that's how long it took the master jade carver and his apprentices to make it, and when he got it—Tlu, that is—he keeled over on the instant in sheer possessive bliss. Why not? Professor Dilthey once said history is the science of inexactly recording human inexact passions, thereby giving birth to sociologists, as every schoolperson knows. Well, let them have a look at all these four-wheeled jade chrysanthemums around here.

B.B., MON HOMMAGE

(à la manière d'épée)

Bela he dead. Hunky. Honky. Too too
late. "It is NOT a qvestion, Billyum,
ov who kin tell
                                        de dancer from de dance—?"
more who can hear the song
                                                                and hear
the four musicians and then hear
him, l'homme, Bela his bohunk mind
behind the song: O Erato!
                                                            Erato,
Thought of my Thought (Ms. Holiday
to you)
              who so deaf can hear the 6th
and not crow too, quartetto grandissimo
(29 changes of tempi in the 1st movement!)
the force there, precisely sforza on those
trembling strings.
                                    Or Russell (e.g.,
the 2nd 8 bars "Lulu's Back in Town")
Homme dans le soixantième an de mon
eage
        dans le montage   Om
hommage O Bela, dead & gone—
was in Liguria once and often in
the warm hayfields of Hungary,
                                                                    OM
                                            OM—

"I'VE NEVER SEEN SUCH A REAL HARD TIME BEFORE": THREE-PART INVENTION

Having planted our little Northern Spy at the wrong season,
Having pruned it in trepidation and ignorance, having watched it

Do nothing at all for a month in the drought-burned, weedy
wasteland
Of the front yard—that prefiguring desolation!—now I am
Uplifted truly
By the sapling's big new leaves and its stems lengthening,
And my mind carries everywhere I go this image of a fresh, pale,
green upsprouting
In the form of a fountain, a small, natural, simple fountain:

And having learned at last, from an intelligent and willing young
man
Behind the counter at Superior Sound, Inc., on East Erie Boulevard,
The definitive and conclusive difference between a ceramic and
a magnetic
Cartridge for my stereo turntable,
Having placed this sparkle of knowledge in my mind like a jewel
on a dark velvet ground,
I glance at it hundreds of times in passing, so to speak,
With a little thrill of gratification for its novelty, its actuality,
And especially for its purity, its unfailing, useless betokening
of what is:

And every day these twinges of pain in my heart, that muscle
unenvisionable,
Draining me downward like the "flow of atoms" into cool organic
earth,
The quicksand,
Downward in this strange new fluidity, this impersonal dissolution,
Drawn by an energy somehow inside me and yet not mine—
How stunning the methodical magnitudes of force!—
Make me wonder, somewhat abstractedly, about the pulverization
of the soul,
About vast windy wastes of crumbled joys and drifting knowledge,
and about what becomes
Of all the disjuncted dregs of consciousness:

This song is a wave forever rolling among
the stars.

AMERICAN NYMPHS

CARL RAKOSI

I

From a minor
branch
of the Oceanids,

notes
to The Welfare
Department:

I.

"To whom
it may concern,
I have no
children yet
as my husband
is a truck driver
and works
day and night."

We understand!

II

"Gentlemen,
in answer
to your letter
I have
given birth
to a ten
pound boy.

I hope
this is
satis-
factory."

Zeus himself
couldn't have
done better!

III

"Dear Welfare,
this is
my eighth
child.
What are you
going to do
about it?"

You will hear
in due time
from Oceanus!

IV *The Real Penelope*

"Madam,
I am glad

to report
that my husband
who is missing
is dead!"

V *Attention, Hymen*

"As you requested,
I am forwarding
my marriage
certificate
and my three
children,
one of which
as you can see
is a mistake."

That was
to be
expected!

VI *Dirge*

"This is
to let
you know
that my husband
got his
project cut off
two weeks ago
and I
have not
had any
relief since."

VII *Ode*

"Dear Sirs,
you have
branded
my son
illiterate.
This is
a dirty lie
as I
was married
a week
before he
was born."

A natural
mistake
under the
circum-
stances.

VIII

"To whom
it may
concern,
unless
I get
a check soon
I will be
forced
to lead
an immortal
life."

Threats
will get you
nowhere!

Envoi

Ladies, forgive me.
This was the work
of the cock-eyed muse.

FROM CHIHUAHUA TO THE BORDER

OSCAR MANDEL

FROM CHIHUAHUA TO THE BORDER

What they do out there, the mountains, is stand
stark useless; bleach (but why?) glued to the sun;
not one green hair grows on these rumps nor is heard
one woosh of a wing or grumble of a throat.
The road's a slap at them they don't know how to feel.
They wall us up (driving north) on either side of one
brown prostrate earth, we give them blank for blank,
until oh God who was it winked at them?
You, you, behind my yawn, you femurs,
ribcage, mandibles, sworn friends to me, you
plotting with foreigners, assassins in my house!

No, no, we love you, chime the bones; drive on, drive on.

"Driving north." That was in the year 1959, when my wife-to-be and I spent a summer together in Mexico. The road we took both going and returning was that grim ribbon which traverses New Mexico and Mexico's inland center, arid, dusty, cutting through torpid villages where now and then a policeman directs traffic from the top of a box marked Coca-Cola.

Those were busy poetic years for me. Poetry composed itself in my very sleep. I would leap out of bed to jot down two lines. Altogether, if my reckoning is correct, some twenty years of "inspiration" were granted me—and if, in spite of the inverted commas I have prudently placed around the word, it strikes you as fatuous, bear in mind that the mediocre enjoy the same exaltations as the gifted. The difference appears in the product, the similarity in the invisible passion that made it. Dunces, in short, also leap out of bed inspired. Eventually my imagination, verve, and hopefulness—even my vocabulary—began to slacken and shrink, and I was virtuous enough not to beat the weary mule.

Title and landscape notwithstanding, my poem is hardly *about* Mexico. What it *is* about I have a mind to speak of at some moderate, unoppressive length. But to say "Chihuahua" without mulling over Mexico, and to mull over Mexico without grieving a while over human misery, is proving impossible to me. In a truly *human* being, ethics must precede metaphysics. The ultimates can always wait. Let them do so now the length of a few pages. . . .

I am no lover of picturesque poverty. Holland is my predilection (need I say more?)—and poverty which I cannot relieve merely breaks my heart. I like a plump, green, well-watered landscape in which no one goes hungry and uncared-for in sickness and old age, where the houses are in good repair and freshly painted, the shops paunchy with merchandise, the clothing colorful and neat. Neatness—should a poet admit it?—is my predilection too. No wonder I have not gone back to Mexico for a second visit, though I live next door to it.

I am not blind to the notorious beauties of Mexico. Once one rises onto the great central plateau and enters the realm of the Conquerors, the landscape dazzles, the clouds are arrayed in voluble billows as if to pose for a Master of the Baroque, and this would be paradise were it not for the marks everywhere upon the human settlements of misery, bad health, ignorance, and violence. In Mexico I renew, on the rebound, my (tempered) admiration for the singular achievements of that Western bourgeoisie which we accredited artists have been mauling so efficiently for nearly two centuries. How lustily we have pummeled the "commercial interests"! We men of letters can even boast of having made up a kind of collective John the Baptist to Marx the Redeemer. We preluded on the keyboard for him, and for his Apostles. While we pummel away, however, and clasp the poor to our bosoms—as metaphorically as possible—the poor have the excellent sense to use our pamphlets, money, novels, votes, and agitation only so far as these will help them up into the very middle class we love them for not belonging to. Once there, they gladly tolerate our lampoons, for they had rather be rich and pummeled than poor and patronized.

Here then is one reason why artists are so particularly fond of Mexico. The poor seem somehow more authentic to them, though why a brazier is more authentic than an all-electric kitchen quite escapes me. Not that authenticity (whatever that means) interests me a great deal anyhow. Some finer souls carry their fastidious devotion to the point of adopting these "primitive customs," shedding the "materialistic trappings of our industrial society," and learning to rejoice in crumbling walls, makeshift furniture, homespun rags, and gastroenteritis. They attract the stupefied of their barefooted neighbors, who, endowed with sense instead of genius, regard them as harmless loonies and continue to hope, pray, sometimes work, and if possible steal in order to buy plastic goods (long live plastic goods) and large automobiles.

The genuine beauties of Mexico, apart from its natural scenery, are mostly the legacy of the wicked Spanish occupation, dispossession, and exploitation. As happens so often, beauty and injustice go hand in hand, posing a moral dilemma which no one seems to notice but which has long bedeviled me. It is an inconvenient and unpresentable phenomenon. Good art is usually a child of luxury, and luxury is seldom a child of justice. This is apparent enough in Europe to anyone who cares to reflect upon the socioeconomic origins of almost all its beauties; but the unsavory truth is even more obvious in Mexico, where the Indians—to put it succinctly—toiled unto death in the mines so churches and palaces could be silvered over. In our own proletocracies, democratic or totalitarian, we can speak in a rough and ready fashion of a reliable inverse correlation between social justice and aesthetic achievement. The repulsive but well-meant housing blocks for the masses East and West provide the picture that stands for a thousand words.

Naturally these large human tides do not operate by clockwork, and there are, for reasons amenable to our reason, notable pockets of exception. But my heart goes out to nations or cultures in which an equilibrium of sorts came about between social justice and aesthetic refinement. In Holland, for instance, but also in colonial New England. In these and other places, extreme luxury and beauty were "renounced" in favor of such an equilibrium. Dutch and New England beauty fell short of Italian beauty, but Italian social justice fell short of Dutch and New England social justice. More social justice means less beauty, but that which remains is more wholesome for that very reason. It refreshes the mind without oppressing our thoughts with ideas of slave labor, intense poverty, disease, and Neronism. The ethical and aesthetic reach an accommodation.

I would not care to have these historical ideas of mine examined too minutely. There is something of the useful fiction in them. But also, I hope, of usable truth.

While I was conscious of the wrongdoings of the builders of Guanajuato and Taxco, this did not and does not to this day trigger in me any particular outbreak of love for their victims. I am free of that automatic twitch. We are always supposing that the oppressed are more admirable than their tormentors. But the little I know about pre-Columbian Mexico has failed to give me fits of nostalgia. The cruelties of the Spaniards but superseded the crimes of their victims. Today we hear grisly stories about the systematic extermination of the Amazonian Indians. But I do not turn instantly sentimental over these same Indians, extolling their chants and stories and customs at the expense of our own dirty civilization. A few years ago a white woman emerged from the jungles of the Amazon. She had been captured by an Indian tribe before she was ten years old, had lived with them, had married an Indian, and had remained with them until the day when, fearing for her life in one of the eternal wars which these picturesque and endearing tribes fight against one another, she had finally made her way back to the whites. The perfectly artless account of her life that she gave to some Italian anthropologists was such as to make a sentimentalist break out in perspiration. Amidst a hundred tales of truceless wars and murders in these unpolluted jungles, one episode has settled for good in my mind. A party of Indians is attacked and overpowered by some enemy warriors. The men escape or are killed in combat. The women and girls become prizes (the little white girl among them). But the boys are grabbed by the feet, swung, and their skulls smashed against a tree.

The cruelties of the Aztecs are notorious, and so are those of the North American Indians. I am not refusing to believe that "savages" can live at peace with one another. But so can the Swedes. Naked or dressed, man is an inherently irritable creature and turns amiable only under a certain constellation of external factors (have they ever been named and studied?) which can occur in the jungle, the savannah, or the city. There is, at any rate, no point in beating our civilization with a primitive's stick.

Nor did I fall into an ecstasy over pre-Columbian art. I paid dutiful visits to the pyramids, the temple sites, the ruins, the museums, always "impressed," but seldom imbued with the intense joy I require of art, whether comic or tragic. Pre-Columbian art proved too relentlessly thick, gnarled, grotesque, tormented and ferocious to suit me. These are all authentic *qualities* of course; but it so happens that, mild myself, I like them in moderation, and prefer them set off against fairer qualities—say, a gargoyle on a cathedral; while I am perfectly content when these fairer qualities beckon to me without those of ferocious power. For me, the sweetness, the pity, and the complex intellectual precision sometimes achieved in our advanced civilizations are not to be bartered for the accomplishments of primitive groups, whether in the arts or in matters of wisdom. It is good to know what they have wrought, and it would be stupid to deny that they can give us lessons (as the child can lesson the adult), for every human advance comports some losses, so that a turn of the head backward is never a waste of time—when Sèvres flood the market, an infusion of Papua is healthy—but it is sheer frowardness to hold up the primitive like a cross to lead us into battle.

While lingering among Aztec, Toltec, and Mayan vestiges, I will confess in an aside that I am not your man for even the best of ruins. You will find me walking rather disconsolately amidst heaps of stones, outlines of bathhouses, recesses for kitchens, shattered columns (unless arranged picturesquely by Chance), and segments of pavement. I do not require a few shards of pottery to grow melancholy over the leveling passage of time and the evanescence of things. In Rome look for me not in the Forum but on the Campidoglio, in the evening, when it lies in its tender lights, noble, venerable, harmonious above its stairs, that grand one in the center, the other to the left of it. I had rather study a ruin in a text than sweat over it in the summer sun. After the Campidoglio you can find me with Bernini on the Piazza Navona. Aztec pyramids indeed! Think too of the unbelievable leap from those mountains in northern Mexico to the Piazza Navona. Is there a planet, among those millions of cultured and developed earths which, we are assured, wander the fearful yonders of the universe, wider and wilder than ours in its contrasts?

Many years ago I was walking along the remains of the Roman wall in England, when I met a laborer chipping away at some stones. "What are you doing?" I asked. "Mending the ruin," he replied. Mend away, friend, mend away.

As I write these pages about my summer in Mexico, I discover that I have neither the desire nor the talent to set down the dozens of intimate contours of a voyage, the flavor of a remark dropped by someone in a café, the colors of a marketplace, the juices dripping from a melon, the cry of a parrot, the reek of buses, a good diarrhea in Taxco, the night one sleeps all dressed in a hotel room out of sheer disgust, dinner among the flamingos in Mexico City. . . . No, consult someone else, my patience fails me.

Still, I want to retrieve an experience, on a sunny and windy afternoon God knows where, that showed me the grain of truth in the Romantic vision of the wise, profound, genuine, unlettered therefore unspoiled peasant—a truth admissible only if we complete the picture, and are willing to add the dark colors—the brutalities, the diseases, the vicious superstitions. Be that as it may, Adriana and I drove up a hillock one afternoon, using a hazardous dirt road until it lost itself in a pile of grass; then walked to the top, which was flattened out. The height was modest, yet the prospect all around was ample. We stood on the site of some archaeological diggings into the tombs of ancient kings and their followers. The scientists were absent that day, their shack stood empty—we peeked inside and found it full of books—and the site was guarded by a native, a youngish melancholy man with an inevitable mustache, a wife whom we did not see, a vague but large number of children, and merry chickens. As my wife's Spanish is excellent, and mine passable, we had no problems with our Mexican, who was glad to see a couple of visitors. He was as true and unspoiled and perhaps noble a son of the earth as one could wish to find in a moist travelogue. He spoke in a gentle voice about the ancient rulers. When they died, their wives and their retainers were dispatched for company. He thought this admirable. "If I had a master, I would die with him too," he said (more or less) with simple artless words. Every now and then, as if coming to the end of a paragraph, he would complete a portion of a story with a "según la relación de Michoacan"—so speaks the chronicle of Michoacan—as if to give his tale a certitude which it would have lacked as one man's report. This almost sad refrain has remained with me like a music. Something out of the lungs of human history was blowing over us that afternoon. We sat on one of the funeral mounds, listening to this bard of the earth. He pointed to a cemetery in the distance, abortively surrounded by three walls. A team of officials—from the United Nations, we gathered—had been to the village, and they had scolded the villagers: "Aren't you ashamed to leave your graveyard exposed on all sides; look at the cows, look at the pigs there, grubbing among your dead!" The villagers had been ashamed. They began to build the walls. Then the team left. Three walls were completed, the fourth was never built. The cows and the pigs were still foraging among the dead. It was not very decent. Furthermore the strangers tried to keep the men in the village from drinking and shooting so much. And they built latrines. Once a little girl of his had been very sick. He made a vow to Our Lady up there, far up on another hill—he would crawl on his knees all the way from the village to light candles to her if the little girl recovered. She did. He crawled and crawled. His knees were bleeding.

The afternoon wore on. Our host dabbled in sculpture. His habit was to leaf through the books of his employers, and when he had time he hammered away at the red, porous stone of the region. What he came up with was original; he clearly did not try to copy the photographs, he allowed them to give him ideas—which were authentically Mexican, of course—not Sèvres!—strong ideas and deeply his own after all. We took two of the pieces along; they stand in our garden to this day. As for the world outside, he knew it only by hearsay. He had heard that in the cities—in the capital, for instance—people had houses on top of other people—he had trouble expressing the strange notion of houses several stories high. One day he would go see for himself. . . .

So then I too have spent a few hours on an Aran island, and assured myself that there is indeed a poetry of the people, something beautiful in that it has been generated slowly, "organically," without imposition from that "above" which can be the Intellectuals, or the Officials, or Big Business—we feel it at once to be as true as the call of an animal. If we do not romanticize this poetry and this wisdom, we are allowed to say that something precious is lost when we move on, and we are allowed to turn our heads backward and sigh. But to give up our knowledge of the atom's structure, to give up Bach, to give up the Campidoglio in order to return to the folk, such a thought is monstrous. For myself, I am so far gone that I would not even give up my French sauces and wines for the beauties of primitive existence. And finally, if I admired the Mexican man on the hill, it was not in order to forget that we too counter our gas-chamber rabble with a host of "beautiful souls." Simple cultures produce them, and refined civilizations produce them.

In the capital we had rented an apartment for a month on the fourth "house above house" of a new building, never quite finished and already crumbling, like all the ambitious technological goods of poor countries. One evening a mouse jumped out of the oven door just as my wife was bending over to start the evening meal. The elevator did not work and perhaps never would. We were young and sturdy and could manage the ups and downs with ease, but we worried at first about the rubbish disposal. On the appointed day, however, a little girl appeared, not quite as tall as the trashcan and thoroughly undernourished. Filled with pity and shame, but freezing my impulse to carry the load for her, I watched her drag it painfully out the door and down the stairs. Anything else would have been impertinent. She would not have thanked me. This was her appointed task. A coin or two might be had from it, dutifully delivered to her father, the concierge. Vacationing foreigners should not break in with outlandish charities. There and elsewhere (giving half-eaten rolls to beggars and the like) I also learned the rule that where misery is the rule, the well-to-do must stiffen against compassion or be annihilated by it. Misery besieges them on every side, day after day; and what is the good of confessing, "I am one of the oppressors"? This may work in the long run, it may be historically significant and useful, it may help change the nation for the better, and therefore such recognitions should be abetted, but on a Thursday afternoon, when the hundred and fifty-fifth hungry child of the week begs you for money, what do you do in order to survive yourself? What does even a revolutionary do as he crosses the town amidst the crippled beggars, the deformed old men sleeping on benches, the mothers picking at the refuse of a restaurant? He too waves them aside. Or no longer sees them.

Here nevertheless a meanness of mine comes to haunt me again. We had dined in the company of another young couple in a restaurant where some mariachi players were performing—odious music!—and felt a crescendo of vexation at the well-organized extortions practiced upon us by the management. The charges were outrageous, the extras cropped up on every side, and when it was all over we left in a sullen mood. My car was parked near the entrance. The uniformed doorman hurried up to it and performed his minor duties. I took in his pathetically baggy trousers and ill-fitting tunic—what is more abject than a *grand gala* uniform three sizes too large?—and the look—what shall I say?—not of tragic suffering—no, simply pain and resignation when I angrily ignored his outstretched hand and drove away. The face showed in the rearview mirror for a second, perfectly void of anger. My own evaporated at once. I wanted to drive back, but could not bring myself to turn the car around, explain to my wife and friends, and issue regally to bestow a gratification on the poor devil. . . . How often, and for how many years, the image of that shabby *chasseur* has come back to reproach me. Was it his fault they were cheating me inside? None of their wicked gains trickled down to him.

At the end of our summer in Mexico, we drove north out of Chihuahua one morning before breakfast, and stopped at a restaurant midway to the border. There we got our last grime and peeling walls, and took our last prudent measures—no water, no butter, no milk. Then into the desert again, the vast beautiful horror of which my poem is a memory, and then, unbelievably, Texas—I think it was Texas—or was it New Mexico? And that time only, never before and never after—an exaltation of patriotism swelled in my ribcage. I could have kissed the asphalt. We halted at a bright chromium-and-plastic "Eats," drank the water, spread the butter, poured the milk, and marveled after three months at the smiles and the cleanliness. Ah, those Indians are not a cheerful race! They are not poor in the Neapolitan way. Here was my white-toothed America again, "Hi folks, what'll it be?"

One surge of this love of America has taught me for the rest of my life the visceral reality of such attachments; I can now reproduce the emotion of a Yank in Asia who gets news of the latest baseball score. If I were a novelist, I would not need notebooks filled with a hundred "real experiences." Imagination's business is to make do with one.

Although we know how moth-eaten the ancient distinction between the soul and body is, we cannot help continuing to feel it, and therefore to entertain a kind of hostility toward these bones and guts and fibers which sustain and indeed create our consciousness, and then extinguish it. In this support and sustenance, they are at one with that portion of Nature—the earth—which feeds and oxygenates us, and then kills and buries us. In all strictness of thought, my poem could have chosen the green hills of Northumberland as aptly as the brown mountains of Chihuahua, but the feeling of death transpires more easily from the latter, and the bones seem to be more at home there. In that setting my spirit feels more forsaken, embedded in the body, which in its turn is embedded in the bleak universe, than it does where the birds give their specious gaiety to the scenery and the saps fool us for a while into delusions of friendliness.

As I see it, we are as right to distinguish between spirit (or soul, or mind) and body as to discriminate between lungs and stomach. I am aware that spirit is thought, that thought is (almost exclusively) language submuttered, and that language is an "electrochemical" activity of the brain. I place that term between slightly ironical flicks only because in another generation or two some other word will be in fashion. The argument will remain the same, however: mind and flesh are both made of the same "natural stuff." But this kinship does not prevent them from engaging in frequent civil wars, simply because each organ of each organism seeks to maintain its own coherence, vigor, and life. It has "its own interest at heart"—that of surviving, yes, but more specifically, that of continuing to play its own game: digesting, breathing, squirting hormones, and the rest. The brain's characteristic game (I mean that portion of the brain which is most properly human) is to think, and our desire for immortal life is little more than the brain's urge to persist in its own inherent function. Its dislike of death corresponds to the stomach's resistance to rancid food. The stomach expresses itself through certain contractions and secretions of chemicals, the brain through its alarmed and defiant thoughts.

One of these thoughts is that thinking is a product of the all too mortal brain. Another is how much lovelier it would be for our thinking if thought were an eternal, distinct, insubstantial substance (called "spirit") which only transiently condescended to occupy a room in our house of flesh. What a benefit to homeostasis that would be! Nor should we wonder that, if the brain emits thought, it also emits thought about thought, which is but another thought. Why not? The poem, in short, continues to stand under the "one substance" view of the universe: it does not imply a radical division between body and soul.

The *feelings* in which these thoughts bask take us even deeper into the "one substance" philosophy. All our feelings can be sorted out into the two categories of pleasure (favorable) and pain (unfavorable). If we translate this into a primal attraction and repulsion, we realize, perhaps with a shock, that even our most human emotions (resentment, for example) unite us, not only with the most primitive organisms, but with the entire universe, alive or unalive. For the inorganic is also constituted and agitated primordially through attraction and repulsion, the going toward and the distancing from. Step by step up the chemical ladder of complexity, this to and from becomes, in living organisms, pleasure and pain, and eventually affection and hostility—and we could write a fairy tale in which the negatively charged particles rushed toward the positively charged particles with a feeling of love!

But what is the ultimate and irreducible reason for the attraction and the repulsion of two units of the universe? What is the final physical explanation? After what reason given can no further reason be asked? And: are these questions unanswerable? If so, why so?

The scientific method itself, which has my full allegiance, suggests that *any* human concept of the universe collapses at the outermost edge. The totality of the universe is not even *theoretically* apprehensible by means of the senses we possess and the equipment we manufacture to stretch our senses. We know that even though we may be wanting a few senses, having three or four more would still keep Kant's Thing-in-itself out of our reach, assuming that anything can be conceived of as being in itself. Furthermore, our radical inadequacy to the universe stares us in the face as frankly as a brick wall. Our notions of time and space lead us to a ridiculous dead end at the limits of the universe. Scientists shrug their shoulders. It is none of *their* business, they say. Well, whose business is it? Philosophers know even less about it, and surely you will not ask your local archbishop? Science pursues time, space, and causation as far as its legs will run, and then turns around and runs back. For the ultimate questions are unanswerable not because we fail to see sharply enough; not because mathematicians have yet to discover the formulas; and not because our instruments need more refinement. The ultimate questions are not in the same category as, for example, the question how many grains of sand there are in the world, which is only "technically" unanswerable. No. The ultimates take us clear across the barrier of Nature as man can conceive it forever and ever from the "prison" of his own nature. This is what I mean when I say that man is *radically* limited. From which it follows ineluctably that something in the universe is itself radically *other* than "electrochemical forces" or whatever name we choose for our "one substance."

But what if this concept of radical otherness were to be applied to our consciousness too?—strange as it may seem that otherness should give a sign of its existence not only at the confines of causation, time, and space, "where words fail us," but pat in the middle of our own "living rooms," if I may so express it.

At the heart of this supposition is a distinction which I have purposely blurred up to this point, because it is not required for the poem: the poem makes sense strictly as the clash between two members of the same ontological club—an ontological civil war, in short. But now let us make trial of another idea: *thought is other than consciousness*. Even thought about thought is separable from consciousness. We say quite sensibly that we are conscious *of* thought, whereby we correctly imply that these two events are distinct. Thought (like feeling) is the "electrochemical" activity of a specific organ and as such belongs to the world of time, place, cause-and-effect along with the rest of the body; whereas our consciousness of thought and feeling appears to escape from that universal net.

I say *appears* to escape. For concerning consciousness, the first mystery is, is there a mystery?

Sometimes I am moved by philosophers and scientists who deny the otherness, the mystery. Perhaps "consciousness" is simply a word we happen to use for yet another activity of matter—or another function of energy—for example the scanning that one portion of the brain performs upon another. But perhaps this is not enough. And then I am moved by those who feel that this "internal illumination" (the expression has been ascribed to Einstein) is *other.*

Yet to ask what this otherness consists in is futile. We know only that our human constitution leaves us helpless to answer questions which that very constitution poses. Discourse takes us to a certain faraway point, and then a black hole swallows it: it vanishes. Every conceivable geometry of space—bent, returning upon itself, and so forth—remains inside the unbreachable prison of our "categories," to use Kant's term. But these categories are not Romantic inventions of ours or accidents implanted in us. Everything we know about the evolution of living creatures implies that all of them, including man, adapt themselves to conditions laid out before any life existed in the universe. Does the earth's atmosphere happen to let certain wavelengths through to the surface while barring others? Very well: our organs conform by seeing the ones and not seeing the others. By the same token, we do not impose the categories of time, space, and causation on the universe. The universe imposes them on us—if we want to live. We have inherited from the lowliest bacterium a humble subservience to these categories. Therefore time and space, and the chaining of events under them, can be thought of as the conditions that sprang out, with the Primal Explosion, from the radical otherness that was itself neither time nor space. Better still, they can be regarded as *constituting* the Primal Explosion, so that *they were* and *the universe was* are synonyms; while the question how that otherness sparked, or converted itself into, our very own universe must remain buried, since only our side of the tracks, so to speak, can be explored.

I am arguing here—with much trepidation—that a similar *other-*

ness faces us as soon as we separate consciousness from the thoughts and feelings which can and do exist without it, in animals, in infants, and very often in full-grown men and women. Consciousness, like time and space, seems to have one foot (so to speak) in our world of matter and energy, and the other in unutterable strangeness.

Specifically, consciousness, if it exists, is an absolute terminus. I mean: it causes nothing. It is itself obviously caused by the matter/energy of the human brain when the latter is functioning at high capacity, when we say of it that it focuses, or attends. But, uniquely among all known phenomena, it is an effect without ever being a cause. We might think of it as the useless, luxurious "humming of the machine"—provided we allow this humming to be an unutterable strangeness, since, unlike the sound waves produced by ordinary humming, it produces no effect whatsoever. Or again: we can call it the clarity in which we dwell when thoughts or feelings peak. At a certain peak of activity, the "veil is rent" (the veil that obscures the thoughts and feelings of animals, of infants, and often our own)—and the electrochemical forces are transfigured.

Remember that, even as I write these words, I remain in doubt. Is this supposed illumination but an "aspect" of neuronal activity? But all aspects of all things are co-equal perceptions that strike us (directly or through instruments) in parallel or convergently. Thus at one moment we see a rose as a beautiful flower, at another as a heap of atoms. These indeed are aspects. But while our instruments are able to catch the chemistry and electricity of our thinking and feeling, so that we can in a real sense perceive them, neither they nor our senses can catch our consciousness of these thoughts and feelings, since consciousness is incapable of acting upon any instrument. We are conscious of setting up the instruments meant to catch our consciousness, but conscious of their capturing only that which we are conscious of (namely thoughts and feelings). So perhaps this consciousness is not a mere "aspect" that we can perceive alongside other aspects. It is as though a butterfly were holding the net that is meant to catch it. Never can we get *in back* of this consciousness: it is always itself in back.

Nor is it easy to account for the oddity of consciousness by treating it as an emergence. An emergence is a quality or property of a highly complicated system which the parts of the system cannot produce *until* connected together as a system. We know that adding items to a system can sometimes do much more than merely make the system bigger. At a certain point, quite startling and unexpected properties emerge. And this seems for a moment, philosophically speaking, an adequate approach to consciousness, which undoubtedly emerges at a certain point of accretion and complication in our billions of neurons. Yet again, emergent properties *behave;* they have detectable effects; they are part and parcel of the electrochemical realities; while consciousness remains (it would seem) half in and half out of these realities. Therefore, though still teased by my doubt, I continue.

Consciousness is of thought, emotion, perception, and volition. We may think of it as their implosion, or glow, or mirror, or even receptacle, though all such terms are necessarily lame. They are lame, of course, because they necessarily belong to our "electrochemical" world; we have no "strange" terms from that "other" realm with which to describe it. We are certain only that consciousness does not disturb the world. Having no effect whatsoever, it is not subject to measurement, experimentation, alteration. We know how to snuff it out (nothing, alas, is easier), without knowing what it is. It can be left out of all scientific observations: perfectly and unalterably passive, it is incapable of modifying a result, it is never even an infinitesimal factor neglected only for practical reasons—it is a perfect zero in the world of material energy in which we move. And it has no "survival value" for the species. No wonder, says Teilhard de Chardin, that it has been ignored by science. It exists—we "see" it—but it does not behave. More: its existence is the central event of our lives. For when we say that we want the self to survive, we do not mean the mere thought, "I am I," or "I am John Doe," but the implosion of clarity in which the thought swims: the consciousness of self.

One charm of this point of view is that it does not smuggle free will into our behavior. Consciousness has nothing to do with the will except to register it. Volition, like emotion and cerebration and perception, proceeds in its world of material energy. It is subject to the ordinary laws of cause and effect, and is easily conceivable without its conscious reverberation, such as we guess it to be in animals and such as we know it to operate very often in ourselves.

All one can say is that our illusion of free will probably derives from our helpless thoughts concerning our consciousness.

To argue that consciousness is perfectly passive is not to decry or deny our vaunted ability to make our minds control our bodies—to some extent, Man has always known that such control can be exercised, and this knowledge can be validated in spite of the superstitions and charlatanisms which have always polluted the "mind over matter" phenomenon. But the point is that this control refers us to thought, not to consciousness. And our thoughts are "electrochemical." So viewed, the impact of mind on matter appears as an entirely plausible interaction (within limits) of two elements belonging to the same ontological club. The stomach can act on the brain, and the brain can act on the stomach. Consciousness attends, but is irrelevant. Quite incidentally, I do not believe that thoughts can move billiard balls (and the like) any more than I believe that our stomachs can.

Does thinking exist without consciousness? It clearly does. True, our most complex cerebrations are necessarily conscious, for when the brain works above a certain threshhold of intensity, it generates consciousness—what I have called the humming of the machine. But we guess that animal thinking fails to cross that threshold, we are all but sure that infant thinking is unconscious, and we know that crowds of unconscious thoughts crisscross our brains not only when we sleep but in our waking hours too. We know it—without the help of psychoanalysis—because now and then a few of these thoughts intensify suddenly enough to awaken our consciousness. As we become aware of these specific thoughts, we also grow conscious of the diffuse magma of thoughts out of which "bubbled" the important ones that sought the light. We cannot seize these lesser thoughts, but they surround the conscious ones like an aura. For the rest, our instruments confirm our individual experience, since they show a great deal of cerebral activity during certain phases of our sleep—thoughts that run helter-skelter over our sleep-loosened circuits, and most of them destined to remain subconscious.

I do not mean, however, that once our thoughts are intense enough to create consciousness, they immediately create *full* consciousness. Consciousness has its degrees; it does not obey an on/off or an all-or-none regulation. It dims and grows brighter before vanishing at one end or reaching perfection at the other—the latter when we concentrate all our thinking on the subject of ourselves: I am I. Hence I easily admit the possibility of a beginning of consciousness—a rudimentary consciousness—in the higher primates, just as it makes a beginning in the child. The guess that animals think without it when they think at all—in images, in smells, in tactile sensations, and so forth—remains reasonable, but a few beginnings of consciousness at the upper limits of primate life are not unthinkable.

As for computers, I am not much troubled by the question whether they will one day be conscious. Since I take our thinking as such to be purely "physical," I do not see why thinking of a sort should not be physically performed by a machine we manufacture for the purpose of thinking. But what results are to be expected from the profound chemical differences between computers and human beings? We already know that their thought-capacity is unlike ours—vastly better in some ways, clumsy in others. It remains for us to wonder whether consciousness—assuming it to be more than a word—is uniquely a property of our proteins, starches, nucleic acids and so on, or whether the components of a computer can generate it too. If they can, welcome! More consciousness can do us, or the universe, no harm. I do not begrudge it to the ape, and have no reason to be afraid of it in a machine.

Inevitably, having come this far, I need to say a word or two about the "mystical" reverberations of these views of mine, however cautiously I hold them. Scientists and philosophers who strongly feel the mystery of it all sometimes keep traveling until they arrive at positions one can call more or less religious. Their opponents suspect them of arriving there chiefly because they wanted or needed consolation. The world is full of tired scientists looking for spiritual refreshment. I, unfortunately, have no refreshment to offer. My tears do not govern my thoughts. The *otherness* we butt against—of causation, of time, of space, and perhaps of consciousness—simply tell me that we animals are not "adequate" to the ultimate universe. We apprehend it as the creatures we are, "provincially." We can proceed to postulate that the number of such epistemological provinces is prodigious, perhaps "infinite." Furthermore they all coexist. They do not abolish one another.

Now, even *a priori* we should think it unlikely that all these realities would exist merely side by side, without the least interference, like parallel slats. No, these beams into reality must cross one another now and then, and here and there—time and space must touch other "dimensions"—and where they do, the creature that stands at the beams' junction receives intimations of the reality beyond its own—or should we say athwart its own? This is where we human beings ask our unanswerable questions. But unanswerable as they are, they do not suggest—alas!—that were an answer forthcoming, it would bring us the consolations we expect from a religion, consolations without which religion does not interest us. In other words, nothing I have said opens so much as a chink through which we might catch a glimpse of a power friendly to us, or the least promise of survival after death. And I can only repeat, with a sigh: alas. I remain as I began, the fear at my throat, in love with my consciousness and cursing it all the while; loving, that is, everything in awareness except the awareness that itself will end. For I know how easily it vanishes in us even while we are alive. A minor relaxation in the physical activity of nervous tissue, an accident, an illness dim it and then switch it off. Here is an event apparently mysterious in its essence yet grossly physical in its origins. Must it die with the body that causes it, or shall we draw hope from the belief that it is in itself uncanny and other? But why should "uncanny and other" amount to an intimation of survival? In the Book of the Universe, the pages we cannot read are probably as bleak of comfort to us as those we absorb. My horror is intact.

Drive on, chime the bones, drive on.

ALPHABET

INGER CHRISTENSEN

Translated from the Danish by Susanna Nied

1
apricot trees exist, apricot trees exist

2
bracken exists; and blackberries, blackberries;
bromine exists; and hydrogen, hydrogen

3
cicadas exist; chicory, chromium,
citrus trees; cicadas exist;
cicadas, cedars, cypresses, the cerebellum

4
doves exist, dreamers, and dolls;
killers exist, and doves, and doves;
haze, dioxin, and days; days
exist, days and death; and poems
exist; poems, days, death

5
early fall exists; aftertaste, afterthought;
seclusion and angels exist;
widows and elk exist; every
detail exists; memory, memory's light;
afterglow exists; oaks, elms,
junipers, sameness, loneliness exist;
eider ducks, spiders, and vinegar
exist; and the future, the future

6
fisherbird herons exist, with their grey-blue arching
backs, with their black-feathered crests and their
bright-feathered tails they exist; in colonies
they exist, in the so-called Old World;
fish, too, exist, and fish hawks, ptarmigans,
falcons, sweetgrass, and the fleeces of sheep;
fig trees and the products of fission exist;
errors exist, instrumental, systematic,
random; remote control exists, and birds;
and fruit trees exist, fruit there in the orchard where
apricot trees exist, apricot trees exist
in countries whose warmth will call forth the exact
color of apricots in the flesh

7
given limits exist, streets, oblivion

and grass and gourds and goats and gorse,
enthusiasm exists, given limits;

branches exist, wind lifting them exists,
and the lone drawing made by the branches

of the tree called an oak tree exists,
of the tree called an ash tree, a birch tree,
a cedar tree, the drawing repeated

in the gravel garden path; weeping
exists as well, fireweed and mugwort,
hostages, greylag geese, greylags and their young;

and guns exist, an enigmatic back yard,
overgrown, sere, gemmed just with red currants,
guns exist; in the midst of the lit-up
chemical ghetto guns exist
with their old-fashioned, peaceable precision

guns and wailing women, full as
greedy owls exist; the scene of the crime exists;
the scene of the crime, drowsy, normal, abstract,
bathed in a whitewashed, godforsaken light,
this poisonous, white, crumbling poem

8

whisperings exist, whisperings exist
harvest, history, and Halley's

comet exist; hosts exist, hordes
high commanders, hollows, and within the hollows
half-shadows, within the half-shadows occasional

hares, occasional hanging leaves shading the hollow where
bracken exists, and blackberries, blackberries
occasional hares hidden under the leaves

and gardens exist, horticulture, the elder tree's
pale flowers, still as a seething hymn;
the half-moon exists, half-silk, and the whole
heliocentric haze that has dreamed
these devoted brains, their luck, and human skin

human skin and houses exist, with Hades
rehousing the horse and the dog and the shadows
of glory, hope; and the river of vengeance;
hail under stoneskies exists, the hydrangeas'
white, bright-shining, blue or greenish

fogs of sleep, occasionally pink, a few
sterile patches exist, and beneath
the angled Armageddon of the arching heavens, poison,
the poison helicopter's humming harps above the henbane,
shepherd's purse, and flax; henbane, shepherd's purse
and flax; this last, hermetic writing,
written otherwise only by children; and wheat,
wheat in wheatfields exists, the head-spinning

horizontal knowledge of wheatfields, half-lives,
famine, and honey; and deepest in the heart,
otherwise as ever only deepest in the heart,
the roots of the hazel, the hazel that stands
on the hillslope of the heart, tough and hardy,
an accumulated weekday of Angelic orders;
high-speed, hyacinthic in its decay life,
on earth as it is in heaven

9
ice ages exist, ice ages exist,
ice of polar seas, kingfishers' ice;
cicadas exist, chicory, chromium

and chrome yellow irises, or blue; oxygen
especially; ice floes of polar seas also exist,
and polar bears, stamped like furs with their
identification numbers, condemned to their lives;
the kingfisher's miniplunge into blue-frozen

March streams exists, if streams exist;
if oxygen in streams exists, especially
oxygen, especially where cicadas'
i-sounds exist, especially where
the chicory sky, like bluing dissolving in

water, exists, the chrome yellow sun, especially
oxygen, indeed it will exist, indeed
we will exist, the oxygen we inhale will exist,
lacewings, lantanas will exist, the lake's

innermost depths like a sky; a cove ringed
with rushes, an ibis will exist,
the motions of mind blown into the clouds
like eddies of oxygen deep in the Styx

and deep in the landscapes of wisdom, ice-light,
ice and identical light, and deep
in the ice-light nothing, lifelike, intense
as your gaze in the rain; this incessant,
life-stylizing drizzle, in which like a gesture
fourteen crystal forms exist, seven
systems of crystals, your gaze as in mine,
and Icarus, Icarus helpless;

Icarus wrapped in the melting wax
wings exists, Icarus pale as a corpse
in street clothes, Icarus deepest down where
doves exist, dreamers, and dolls;
the dreamers, their hair with detached
tufts of cancer, the skin of the dolls tacked together
with pins, the dryrot of riddles; and smiles,
Icarus-children white as lambs
in greylight, indeed they will exist, in-
deed we will exist, with oxygen on its crucifix,
as rime we will exist, as wind,
as the iris of the rainbow in the iceplant's gleaming
growths, the dry tundra grasses, as small beings
we will exist, small as pollen bits in peat,
as virus bits in bones, as water-thyme perhaps,
perhaps as white clover, as vetch, wild chamomile,
banished to a re-lost paradise; but the darkness
is white, say the children, the paradise-darkness is white,
but not white the same way that coffins
are white, if coffins exist, and not white the
same way that milk is white, if milk exists;
white, it is white, say the children,
the darkness is white, but not
white like the white that existed
when fruit trees existed, their blossoms so white,
this darkness is whiter, eyes melt

NINE POEMS

GÖRAN TUNSTRÖM

Translated from the Swedish by Eva Enderlein and Emile Snyder

1

Early morning. Quiet lake.
Deep into space
the mirror image
of the dove
retreats

2

In the middle of the hunting season you change
to a deer
and cross the open fields
I must get down to the water, I am thirsty
Don't kill me, you say
Not again

3
We cultivate the earth together
my brother and I
The soil is so black
The goats leap merrily about
eating hawkweed and grass
My wife is nursing our child by the fire
—Is Cain not coming soon? I am
hungry
And I smile. Her impatience is great

4
Still it is marvelous that you are crazy
tall and wild
and that you were able to borrow wings
that beat against the heavens
I too gain something from it:
I cling to your neck
bury myself in your plumage
We eclipse the moon
Scratch against the constellations
Gone are the calls of the hunting horn and the barking
There will certainly be time for the marriage
to be consummated
before you shake yourself loose
and let me fall
deeper and deeper
into my body
to scrape my skin
against our social security numbers
and the holy mess
the god of psychosis
has compelled you to make

5
All night I have held
a butterfly net over you
It is no longer enough
Your curled upper lip doesn't move me
Nor your dozing by the brim of the sheet
The suspicion has been here since midnight
He has threatened me. He has persuaded me
I have received his pistols
I shall shoot myself into your dreams
Shoot madly into the crowd
on those market squares, where you walk
spreading wishes
I have a nose for your smoke screens
Afterwards you can call the whole justice department
and claim that your husband continues to eat you
It is true. Your create in me
a terrible hunger

6
You say you love red caviar
plastic mugs, both red and blue
old easy chairs and paper clips and pins
broken cliffs and toothless combs
Your love is infinite
Even I am included in your gallery

7
She is a temple without an entrance
Weary or dying of thirst
we have come
                    to the pond smooth as a mirror
She has gathered her shadow

long ago
Why don't we leave?
Once, twice, perhaps three times
she has opened a window to air
her fingertips:
how they glimmered

8

You used to come down in the evening
to drink
The sand is engulfing me
I have gathered my shadow
so that you
when approaching me
in your Syrian-Indian
incredibly beautiful
global dress
remain motionless
as if the world had no axis
and knowledge no center
A few blades of grass on the steppe is all
and never again your mouth against the
cold surface of mine
The dialogue has coagulated
like the herring blood
on the kitchen counter
which, as you can see, I have cleaned up

9

A pair of white wing feathers
lag behind the bird in flight
They still fly
in unison

by will alone
and memory
A faint perception of direction
Each breath
separates them lightly

SAINT ERKENWALD

OMAR S. POUND

In London
not long since Christ
was crossed for Christendom
a bishop blessed the temple haunts
of heathen whores.
His name was Erkenwald,
and *Poules* his church,
re-faithed by him,
they call St. Paul's.
He hurled out idols
or named them newly, Saxon saints,
familiar to his flock.
He bundled out the randy retinue
of Hengist's hordes,
and swore to build the Church anew
to welcome back the Lord.

He hired rough-masons,
each crewed to haul and hew,
and master-masons
with lads to twit and tease
and hone, and cheer the chisels on.
Then, marshalling men of brawn
with belted bellies,

pick and pole probed ruin's mound
to found Christ's firmest foothold in the land.
And there, deep down,
poles poked, picks stuck and snapped,
they'd struck a marble tomb.
"Sarcophagus,"
the clerics said,
garnished with gargoyles,
with lumps where they lacked,
garnet eyes and agate tongues,
and round the tomb letters,
some silver, some gilded with gold.
The Dean thought them Latin, others Greek,
two bundled the letters in lots
till heads were in heat,
and saw many a word that wasn't.
One read the writings of Thor.
A few thought them odd,
with no meaning at all.

Wives plucking pigeons
and whispering awe,
elbowed forward
for more of the marvel,
which, wound round with wonder,
soon spread,
"Sir Kofagus has been found gelded, on a litter of gold."

Lads leapt from learning
turners tossed tools aside
all vied for a viewing
from a dray nearby.

Then beadles and burghers
all breathless and bossy,
bellies an asset in parting the crowd,
cried out clearly, "The Clerk of the Works is here.
"Move over!
Make way for his muster and mare!"

And pushed women aside
with their parsley and wares,
proud to be first to peep inside.
"The lid must be lifted and laid just here. . . ."

So crowbar and jemmy jostled the joints,
Some swore and sweated like clay,
others advised and orated,
till silenced, dismayed:
"A corpse is there, buried, and undecayed."

Look how he lies! Face freckled, nostrils hairy,
flesh unfaulted, unfrumenting, unwormed,
and those cheeks!
Might have swallowed the sun!
Eyes lightly lidded, a falcon at rest,
brows brown and bushy,
chin covered in down.

A girdle of gold gripped the groin,
acorns, falcons, yarrow and lilies
embroidered the cloak
with devout short stitches closely sewn.
New silk on wool,
hood edged with ermine whiter than shell,
linen well laundered,
not a flea in the folds
of the wormless weeds,
flesh unfaulted,
as I mentioned before,
and deeds?
Still unsorted out by the Lord.
"Send for the Bishop,
town troubles
truant trickery
maybe a miracle,
any excuse, but bring him back quickly."

Three messengers, packed up and off, heard

Erkenwald was last seen,
eastward-bound,
to care for morals (some said)
in an Essex nunnery, near Witham, I think.

Lightly loaded they soon caught him up,
what with his walnuts, cheese and new pestle,
but "Erk," as the kitchens called him,
hurried them back:
"We've a vigil tonight,
I'll follow tomorrow.
"Take Broomwit the Beadle
to tone down town tensions till I get back."

At dawn, the abbess, with blessings,
her own white horse,
herbs, honey and ale,
bustled him off to London.

Now Broomwit,
worthy and waiting as ever,
had serviced their lips with awe.
No use!
When the Bishop dismounted,
all shouted, "Good old Erk!"
with a catcall or two from the dray nearby,
as ostlers brought water, a blanket and hay.
A quick blessing . . .
then prayers and some sleep.
But tired in marrow,
visions vied with his vigil
as faith unfurled
a view of the dead in a Heathen world,
where,
deprived of all senses
no river-mists,
no toll of the bell,
no garlic fritters,
no faithful foregathered,

they must be in HELL.
"Dead,
without decay,
body uncorrupted. . . ."
"If Christian,
how come the delay?
"O Magnum Mysterium. . . . But wait!
Is he dead?"
For in death all knowing dies,
and only what we cannot know
proliferates.

Ere vigil and visions were lost, Matins rung,
all gathered for Mass in the autumn sun.

More blessings, (more meaning now),
Chepeside filled
as the choir hallelujah'd
its way to St. Paul's.
"His two favorite rites," a burgher said,
"An Erkenwald blessing, and a Mass for the Dead."

"Beloved Beacons of the Lord," the Bishop began. . .
then stopped.
"He loves your loud laughter,
but, dearest friends, is a Soul lost?"

Mass over,
he turned to the corpse to talk.
Lid lifted, he shortened his sleeve,
thumbed each eyelid up,
till leadened by light they lowered.

"Dear Doers in Christ. . .
"Nought's known but a heathen was buried here.
"If Christian we'd know
birthplace,
marriage,
and death,

but a Heathen. . .
                                        "Who cares?
"Uncaught by chronicle,
        all who might remember him
                                        have melted into Mystery.
"O Magnum Mysterium et admirabile sacramentum."
His arms practiced preaching
                                        while his tongue took a rest.
"Out with it, Erk,"
                                        piped up Pete,
"Ask who he was.
                "If he ain't dead, he oughta know that."
"Oh, Pete,"
                said the Bishop,
                                        "Don't tangle your tenses."
and coughed:
                                "Who were, er. . . , who are you?
"The world's weight.
                                        "What corner did you bear?
"How long, and why here?
"Your wealth?
                                "Whose was it?
                                                        "Who has it now?
"And, er. . . , your Faith?
"How near to Hengist's hordes or Jesus' joy?"

"What light!"
                                the corpse replied,
                                                        and with that!
Tom darted out to tell Chepeside and Molly,
            "That damned body answered the Bishop back!
                                "Erk's right after all! A miracle!
"That means more faithful to our fair,
        our takings up,
                and tithings, too.
"More graves to dig,
                new thongs for sandals,
real relics this year, not fakes,

more mead
and
lots more Molly."

The baker and brewer (brothers) heard Tom.
"Alert the lads!
"More saffron in the buns,
more salt and seasonings to feed their thirst.
"Off that dray, you louts.
"We'll need it now
for those we parch in service of their Lord.
"Pilgrims must pay for piety.
"That Bishop's still braying,
'O Magnum Mysterium,'
a miracle perhaps to fools,
but deeds like these come easy to the Lord."

The Bishop beamed,
"Indeed, all things come easy to the Lord,
when the Prince of Paradise unlocks His Might."

The corpse sighed. . .
"Don't fret,"
said the Bishop,
"We'll soon have you out,
but I'm not sure how."

Said body, "If I knew the world's weight
I'd tell what I bore,
but none knows another's burden,
save the ass.
"How long here?
"Any man's number might guess it right,
800 years perhaps,
but I knew from the grave Christ's birth,
the earth warmed up
and violets grew.

"Who am I?
"Who knows?
"No one cares!

"Your records won't show,
I used them enough to know that.
"My wealth?
"No joyless needs,
I wanted less than I had.
"Possessions possessed me now and then,
with half my life spent
attaching my heart
to this and that,
the rest, detaching it again.
"I was a visiting judge,
town to village, from horse to inn
and back to horse again.
"Forty years,
I ordered my life to public time,
keener than kings for justice.
"Mistakes here and there,
errors from haste,
but none begged my mercy,
my justice sufficed.
"No bribes,
(just once, but who, even you, says 'no' to a king?),
my rank just grew.
"Rich paid what they owed,
the poor, gifts—mostly small—
cummin and leeks,
or nothing at all.
"The day I died, what a day to remember!
"All grieved my going.
"Fogs fouled all that November.
"They furled me in furs,
('His body's cold, but perhaps not dead. . . .')
more like a Master of Merchants than Law.
"They robed me in mantles,
'His rulings were just,'
sandaled my feet, 'Think of those miles
bout a sheep or some logs.
'He never faltered on his way to the Gods.'
"Their love let me live when I wanted to die.

"Embalm me they would
    but terebinth,
        the stuff they soak the linens in,
            was short that year—not merely costly.
"On embalming, the truth:
they decide whose corpse will be uncorrupted,
                while still alive,
then dig you up.
        'Look! A Saint!
            'His body's whole!'
"A cruel sort of logic to play with a soul."

"Oh, yes. . . er. . . , your soul," said the Bishop,
"Is it still stored?
"A man whose faults can be counted
                should surely be saved."

The corpse groaned,
"When I died
        blessings blossomed.
"But now,
        soaked in sorrow
            girdled in grief
                I can't even be kind.
"Lobbed into Limbo, my body lies.
"What worth my wisdom without belief?
"I died
    a pagan
        unbaptized."

Erkenwald wept,
tears brushed the brow of this man of law,
fungus grew,
maggots squirmed,
dust buzzed like the bees
    as Bliss seized a soul
        and corruption its form.

Three years later,
the winter we all lost our bees,
April the Thirtieth, in 693,
Erkenwald died, of chest fever,
as many do,
attending each other's funerals.
March thinned him so, and even Spring
failed to luster the bones or brighten skin. . .
but the earth warmed up
and violets grew.

They buried him Monday,
market day it was,
Each limb wrapped in linen,
his own Coptic comb,
new sandals from Pete,
a wool alb from Witham,
a girdle of gold from the Chepe;
on his heart
his own amber drop,
full of fleas and a fern
in the form of a Cross;
on his head,
an osier crown made by Molly.

And over it all a cloak
embroidered with falcons and flowers,
yarrow and lilies in tiny stitches.
None knew whence it came,
"A gift from a friend for a favor in life."
Who knows?

Broomwit, still waiting and worthy,
puttered and hovered,
scraping grease-marks and smudges,
as coffin was covered
and well-lidded down.

Molly whispered to Tom,
"Will that hold him under?
"Don't want him up and around.
"Might come when it's in,
and he might lose my crown.
"And that heathen the Bishop corrupted
and turned to dust?
"Will he do the same for us?"

Tom's answer was lost as all crowded round
for relics. . .
a sliver of cedar
some lint from his gown.
All envied his ivory comb, twin-edged,
teeth tapered and worn,
but if I know Broomwit,
it's still in the tomb.

Broomwit as ever brushed longings aside!
"Dear Sisters and Brothers.
"Why relics?
"You store in each eye,
Dear Lovers in Christ,
a tear to baptize.
"A relic of Christ in each cleric of God.
"You are your own reliquary.
"All praise to the Virgin Mary. Amen."

Erk always said, "Broomwit's best when caressing a crowd."
The thunder amen'd with the monks,
again and again,
hail flailed the ground,
and freed from a need for relics now,
all solemnly smiled,
wandered off
and withdrew.
One of the deacons put two hairs back,
like Molly's, but who'd know that.

Pete swears Broomwit sighed,
"Relics! The lot of them!
"Begging favors from twigs!"
and left as Pete wept.

To tether this tale:
bells boomed as many and then as one
as Saint Erkenwald joined The Unpaganed One,
name still a mystery,
save to a few,
and to
The Fourth Bishop of London.

Broomwit, even with Spring come alive,
suddenly tired and died.
They buried him
in a tomb, waiting and worthy,
with letters incised in silver and gold:

SERVUS DEI

which is, "Servant of God," I'm told.

THREE POEMS

PAUL CARROLL

THE GARDEN OF EARTHLY DELIGHTS

Suddenly, as if a door in the soul opened, like now,
And you are in it. Here,
On a patch of grass in the park
Near humpbacked Stockton Drive across from the Conservatory
You happen to look at a bush, the leaves
With shapes of tongues of whales
Or tortoise shells, each with almost identical pattern of dull white
As if night with its chalk
Had been making murals; leaves and stems
Supple as gondola poles
Creating a kind of jungle
For the white spider and the ants. While there, above,
Trees bright jade in noonday glare,
No two branches ever quite alike
Like the fingerprints of stars;
While that branch, gesticulating
In abrupt breeze, bald
As if stripped by one of the angels of exile
Who refused to choose between God and Lucifer
And so became a bird.
The grass itself like a lyric by some poet of the T'ang—
Small, and elegant, and tough
Like a marriage that has made it.

"WHAT IS THAT WORD KNOWN TO ALL MEN?"

Our prize blue-ribbon bull Colonies Plaats Jules motionless
As McCormick Place
In the middle of the bull pen, his hide
Of locomotive black-and-eggshell white
A map of Aegean,
The broom of tail a metronome
To flick away the tornado of the flies, his odor overwhelming
As if from one of the Seven Days in Genesis.
I am trying to sit quiet like at Mass
Between Smitty's legs on the tractor seat
As we bounce about slicing
The crust of the cornfield as if it were a cantalope.
I am galloping on Brownie down Giant's Hill between the rows of
 oaks attempting
To elude the ambush
By the bones of the Potawatomi.
I am straddling this hard inner tube of salt
Immense as a monument by Claes Oldenburg, waiting
For Dad to come wading through the deepening waves of dusk
In hip-high rubber boots,
Striped pants and frock coat from the Bank, his grey homburg
Big as Babe Ruth in my brother's card collection,
He'll be puffing on his favorite briar pipe from Donegal, guiding
With the hickory walking stick
The tinkling herd of Holsteins to the salt lick
Where I, whistling, waving, wait.
Fuch is Anglo-Saxon: it means "to plow a field."
With the implication too
"To sow seed in that farrow."

TO MAX JACOB TO PROVE TO HIM THAT I'M A POET

The sun a circus acrobat
Tumbling about the bedroom of the gulls, those waves
Here on the Oak Street beach. And as you always had the patience
to repeat
Joy also can be small
As, say, this tall tan temple
Of a pinecone
I found with my son Luke last week in an empty park in Evanston
That could contain
All of the calendars that the Incas ever made, Max;
Or turn into a library
Of the poems to the swallows that you wrote
Early every morning by your window for a quarter of a century at
Saint Bênoit-sur-Loire
Before strolling over to the old stone church of the Benedictines to
serve as altarboy at Mass.
The pinecone's skin feels prickly—
A little like the photo of Buñuel
As aging, bald grandee with dinner jacket and bow tie black as the
funeral of the sun,
The thick tycoon cigar, the wry grin big as Babylon
As if amused that nobody as yet noticed that those Jesuit semi-
narians in shovel hats and cassocks in *Un Chien andalou*
Being hauled across the floor with the gaggle of dead donkeys
Are really butterflies. Every artist,
Even an atheist from the Middle Ages like Buñuel,
Only serves at the High Mass of reality. Still,
It's so easy when we write a poem
To think we carry truth inside a safe-deposit box
We have created; whereas the evidence clearly seems to indicate
That all of us at best are but like fish
Inside the Shedd Aquarium
Of the imagination. The sun also shines at night.
Of course you knew it all along, Max, as far back certainly
As No. 7, rue Ravignan, Montmartre, your room as blind as Joyce,
the smoking lamp forever lit,

Where on the 7th of October 1909 your Seigneur Jesus Christ in
yellow robe within a watercolor landscape thumbtacked to the
wall, explained
The Tierra del Fuego of the heart, and you
And the other two, who probably were angels, laughed
With the happiness of animals. Max,
I hope you wore that old flea market opera hat on your First Communion Day;
And that your godfather Picasso drew a sun for you
Small as a snail
And elegant as Sanctifying Grace
Which sounds, they say, something like the bottom of the ocean
When the ocean has a mouth.

FOUR POEMS

DEBORAH FASS

1

Oyster without pearl dreamless
void of sleep darkness
separation a lover's
world

2

Seated and staring
in fixed pose of childhood blue TV
tube eyes collect intricate collage.

Pulse of alternating current.
Bones commemorate water upright
chronic state of muscular
tension evolve
into adulthood.

Face or billboard moving
feet street globe.

3
Daily weight of shortened
life span a dull
pressure on abdomen push
on shoulders caved
chest tedious heart body
a bow tight
and arrowless

4 WINTER FOREST

Tree eye mind memory grit
in pocket of sweatshirt illusion
of beach, heart
an inflated balloon on a long line
tugging.

ST. EUSTACE

CARL LITTLE

Any good-sized body of water
always has a wind or spirit of wind
traveling its surface, no matter
how still the day. At least that is
one man's theory as he circles
a hole of water one valley over
from his house. Even surrounded by thick woods
a current of air, a movement
makes him kneel at the edge
for a closer look.
If not denying his own stagnancy
—unacknowledged but present as a bruise
long in healing—
he is surely conjuring up the lost,
giving them a home, however inhospitable.

Studying an etching once, where
the souls of a dead city fled in aimless exodus
on roads through the night, he recalled
the fevered rush of his evenings after work.
The subway's rumbling through the tunnels
must unleash stray winds. Stirred up,
now visible, the gusts streamed
up and down the streets like demons

ripping awnings, tearing off facades
with rage and glee.

The last of a stand of dried reeds
gives the lowest rattle; it causes in the man
an involuntary shudder. Death
brushing by, according to some.
Another, at that moment, might look up
expecting to find, as St. Eustace had,
a stag bearing the crucified Christ
between its enormous antlers.

The man in question simply gets up
and walks away. His supposition—
that any sizable watering place
should have an overseer—
has been proven: a shiver has struck him
in an isolation he has, after all, gone hunting for.

BROTHER WOLF

HAROLD JAFFE

Molly's in the cramped elevator with dirty yellow walls. It stops abruptly at a lower floor and an old man with a tattered coat and red watchcap pulled low over his ears steps inside. The old man is using his thumb to rub the opaque film from his lottery ticket. His hands tremble. The elevator stops again and a pale man with a nervous manner steps in. Runs a pocket comb through his thin dry hair.

Rain outside. Molly waits to cross the Artery. White cars, long trucks. She waits but can't get across. Has to walk to the overpass. Beneath the overpass, near one of the buttresses, V's OD'd again, sprawled on the pavement, couple of kids bent to him.

Leaning against the railing on the overpass, Loraine and F are fixing. Loraine has a yellow leatherette belt around her arm. F just got back from the Rack. Molly nods, walking past.

The Artery dips into the tunnel that cuts through the business loop. Molly enters the tunnel, walking on the narrow pedestrian strip. Whoosh of speeding cars, trucks. Exhaust clouds. The strip is full, M is there, Lois.

Lois to Molly, "You have?"

Molly shakes her head no.

"I got coin," Lois says.

"Don't have," Molly says.

Traffic's loud, Lois can't hear.

"Don't have," Molly shouts. "Try Wolf."

"Wolf has?" Lois shouts.

Molly nods.

Kids on the railing, against the tunnel walls. A boy Molly's seen but don't know squeezes her tit, grins. She keeps walking. Magda's going down on a john, squatting on spike heels in one of the shallow doorways. Leni and R are making out against the railing. Both wear headsets, Leni's sort of nodding out.

R says to Molly, "Wolf's shit, real tasty."

Alone against the railing is the Tattoo Prince. Just about everyone has homemades on their bodies, but Prince is full of them, back and front. His face too. He nods.

"Hello, Prince," Molly says, slipping her headset into place. She's into the sounds as she leaves the tunnel. The Artery widens to eight lanes. Still raining. She's just about lost her in. She'll need a boost by the time she gets to P. She turns up the volume.

She's walking on the strip along the Artery to P. It was P's scam and Wolf thought it would work. Scamming Molly's father. Molly thinks of her father as she passes one of his affiliate buildings, glass and steel, recessed at the center, sort of jutting out at the top. He has a suite in another one just like this, high up, looks out over the city. Her father and mother live apart, but he kinda likes Molly. They hardly ever meet though. Last time was about a year ago in his penthouse suite. He brushed her head and gave her coin. Molly and P were in real tasty with that coin. Not for that long though.

The scam'll keep them in for a long damn time. Except she's needing now and the sounds ain't working either. A john brakes his car and shows coin.

"I won't hump," Molly says.

He nods.

She does him for coin. In his white car on a utility road.

Moving again she sees D who sells her some. She wants to wait for P, do it with him. She don't know if she can wait.

When P mentioned the scam Wolf said, do it. Tap the old man. He makes out he loves his daughter, test him. Will he stick his hand in the vault for his daughter? Will he stick both hands in? Will he stick them in up to his elbows? Let him take a tax write-off. He must have that stip in his policy, kidnapping loss.

That's Wolf.

Molly smiles. But she is scared a little. Or maybe it's just she's low, needing. She thinks of sticking. Just something till she gets to P. That's what she does. Stops off in a toilet, waits for a stall, sticks some. Others fixing and she thinks, maybe, but she don't have her kit. P has it. So she just sticks some above her wrist. Small boost, hold her till she gets to P.

Still raining. She stops at a newspaper stall and buys a paper that she puts on top of her head. A truck sprays water on her. Someone says her name. Fritz.

"Molly."

"Hey, Fritz."

"Here, girl."

Fritz is away from the rain, sprawled on the pavement, leaning against a building. He just fixed, it's in his eyes. He takes the paper from Molly's head and pulls her down next to him. He starts to read the sopping newspaper aloud, saying words like Circuitry and Private Sector and Network and Exxon and Prayer . . .

Fritz reads these words in an exaggerated way, grinning. Then he says, "I heard. You and P gonna try and scam your old man?"

Molly looks at him.

"What happens if it don't work?"

Molly shrugs.

Fritz grins. "What you got to lose, right?"

Molly nods, gets up, continues walking. Only without the newspaper on her head. Raining kind of hard. She turns up the volume on her headset.

P is waiting for her. They kiss. He looks wasted.

She nods yes before he even asks.

They fix in one of the shooting cellars, use P's works and Molly's lucky belt. When they use Molly's laminated blue vinyl belt it usually means a tasty in.

This time it don't work all that good, it's an okay in, that's about it.

Leaning against one of the water pipes in the cellar, P says, "Me and Wolf did the letter."

He hands Molly an envelope with her father's name and address on it. Inside, put together from newspaper print:

We have your daughter Molly and will kill her unless you give us what we demand. Five hundred thousand dollars must be left in front of the Getty Affiliate #3 on East Artery and Seminole. Exactly at six am on

Thursday 24 May, the money in a transparent bag should be placed on the concrete step that leads to the generator room on the north side of the building. We will be in touch with you again soon.

Molly nods, hands it back to him.

"Is it strong enough?" P says.

"I guess."

"Wolf said it had a better chance of working if we made it real strong, but not crazy strong. Maybe I should have said more about how you would be hurt—I mean about what would happen to you if he didn't come up with coin."

"Maybe."

"Yeah. Well I'll make it stronger the second time. He should get this tomorrow. That's the 22nd. The next night me and Wolf'll spell it out for him."

"What'll you say?" Molly says.

"What?"

"About what you'll do to me if he don't come up with the coin."

"Yeah. Well I'll say that we'll shoot you in the back of the head and dump you in a rad-fill.

"Big deal."

"I'll say we'll cut off your arms."

Molly smiled. "That all?"

"I'll say we'll cut off both arms and both titties and send him one of your small pink nipples to prove we mean it."

"Better," Molly says.

"Yeah, well it ain't all that easy coming up with these things. I'll talk with Wolf."

"Old Wolf."

"Right. Which means he'll take a nice cut too."

"So what?" Molly says.

"Right. If the old man gives us what we want we can take care of Wolf. Hey, where'd you get the coin to buy this shit, Mol?"

She don't answer.

"You said you wouldn't be into that shit again, Mol."

"Didn't do much," Molly says. "Hand-job."

"Bullshit. You couldn't buy this shit with what you got from a hand-job."

"You'd be surprised, cowboy. Some johns think I'm worth big coin."

P grins in spite of himself, puts his arms around her. "They're the smart ones."

He tries to kiss her but can't find her lips.

"This is some tasty shit," he says.

"It's getting good," Molly says.

"It's the belt," P says.

"My father gave this belt to my mother before they split."

"No jive?"

Molly and P go to the tower.

When ESSO became EXXON they erected a 97-floor tower with a huge gold-plated replica of the EXXON logo on top. One of the twelve freight elevators was usually left unattended, which is how they got to the top.

Some of the others were there: Magda, Dot, F., Loraine, Long M, Prince. They're all in with some tasty shit Wolf got for them. Long M's only fifteen but he's about six-six, freaky. He hangs out with Sylvie, except Sylvie was sent to the Rack after her fourth OD. Long M gets off on sounds, just about never removes his headset.

Magda is sitting on top of the high railing facing the others. She's almost eighteen, been on her own for about five years. Magda has five sisters, all younger, and all her parents do is work. Which is what everybody else's parents do, except six kids in one family is crazy, especially girls. Magda probably makes bigger coin than both her parents together, only she has a big habit. Also she is good about keeping her friends in. Magda is only a little washed-out looking, blond, with a big chest. Johns dig her. She's been on the strip for a long time, has a whole lot of steadies.

The Tattoo Prince is off to the side by himself.

"Whatchoo got new?" P says.

Prince pulls up his shirt, pointing to behind his left shoulder: a long box, oblong-shaped, with the lid up and what looks like a head inside.

"Tasty," P says. "How the hell you get back there? Must be triple-jointed."

Prince grins.

To F, P says, "Where's Wolf at?"

F shrugs.

"You see Wolf?" P asks Magda.

Magda shakes her head. "Not since he laid this shit on. Want a jolt?"

P and Molly do. They do it away from the wind, using Molly's belt.

"Good. Real tasty," P says. "What's for tonight, Magda?"

Magda shrugs. "Spazzing."

"At the Inst?" Molly says.

"Sure," Magda says.

The Inst is the splay-barn downtown. Live band usually. Lots of sound. Only a few of the kids still danced. Most everyone spazzed, which is sort of spastic, kinda letting it out any-which-way. Real fucked-up.

P mailed the letter to Molly's father, they hung out on the strip, dropped some blueys, then went to the Inst. One of the bike tribes was there bashing some guys. In the center of the floor while the others spazzed. When it was over—the ass-kicking—one of the kids that worked there mopped up the blood and stuff. Bike tribes did this pretty regular and it was almost always over drugs.

Wolf was there but like always there were people around him. He saw P and made the "it's cool" sign with his fingers. P and Molly spazzed until the Inst closed at four. Then they went back to P's lid. Loraine and F were there, coupla others too. F squirted his name and Loraine's on the wall with blood. F was always squirting his blood around after he fixed. Molly and P were going to save their shit for the next day, but they ended up fixing right then and not getting to sleep. Next morning late P went to the strip to make some coin. P had a spazzy look about him and a sort of baby face and the homo johns dug him. Janes too. Molly didn't like the idea of him humping or even doing anything else with janes. Johns weren't that bad 'cause she knew P wasn't getting off on it. She didn't like him with janes.

Molly hung around the lid, watched the tube, slept some. Later she went out to West Artery thinking maybe she'd find that old man who paid her good for a hand-job. But she didn't see him and ended up doing a number with a coupla other johns.

Pretty much all the kids worked the strip, even Loraine who hated doing it. Molly and the others did what they had to do without getting into it, sort of separating themselves. But Loraine never got the hang of this, and after she did a few johns she was always blown out. Loraine was small and thin with long beautiful black hair like velvet, and her being scared and small turned the johns on too. She had a lot of steadies.

Molly and Loraine got to the Inst at about eleven but only F, Loraine's old man, was there.

"Where's P?" Molly said.

F shrugged. "I saw him on South Artery early on. Busy night tonight. Some kind of war going on in the colonies. Johns were full of it."

"What do you mean?" Molly said.

"War," F said. "A small one from the sound of it. I didn't know about it till one of the johns said it. I guess it's on the tube."

"Let's spazz," Loraine said, tugging at F's sleeve.

They went onto the floor. Molly went into the toilet and stuck some shit. Just a little, wasn't top-grade. She went out and spazzed with Long M. Long M kept his headset on real loud even with the live band blasting it.

"Where's P at?" Long M asked.

Molly shrugged.

Magda came in. She gave Molly three or four blueys with some cherry pop.

"Where's P?" Magda said.

"Don't know," Molly said.

"Johns are a little out of it tonight," Magda said.

"That's what F said. I didn't catch it. Something about a war."

Magda laughed. "Want a jolt?"

Molly shrugged. "I'll wait for P."

One of the bike tribes showed up and pretty soon they were smacking around some guys. They were using their chains so it got pretty messy. Then somehow Long M got into the action, like someone pushed him or something, so the bikers kicked his ass too. One of them tore Long M's earphones from his head and splattered the unit on the floor. When the fighting let up Magda and Molly dragged Long M to the side and patched him up a little. It looked like his nose was broke and coupla teeth were chipped. All he wanted was a jolt, which Magda gave him with her own kit.

P never made it to the Inst. Molly went back to the lid but he wasn't there, and some kid who was crashing said that P hadn't been around. It was about an hour before light. Molly went out again, got a ride to South Artery which was where P and the others played rough for coin. From the looks of it that action was still going down. Whole lot of parked cars, johns inside. Other johns walking up and down the strip, some of them negotiating with the roughs. One john was going down on a rough right there, the rough leaning his back on a railing. Molly asked Fritz, who was roughing, about P. Fritz said he was around someplace.

Molly walked for a while longer and then she saw him. P was getting out of a john's sportscar which had just pulled up. He didn't see Molly at first, but then he did.

He put his arms around her. "What are you doing here?"

"What happened to you?"

"Hey, this is big coin, girl. I already made enough to keep us in Wolf's best shit for three, four days."

Molly just looked at him. His eyes looked like he was dropping uppers. He looked beat.

"They made war again," P said. "In the Indian Ocean someplace from what they say. The johns are full of it because for them it means coin."

Molly didn't follow this, but she nodded.

"Which means your old man," P said. "With the coin he stands to make from the war I can't see him griping about laying out a little for his only daughter."

"Let's go back to the lid," Molly said.

P had his arms around Molly's shoulders but he was looking past her.

"Not yet. Still too much coin here. Most action I ever saw here."

"What are you doing?" she said.

"Huh?"

"You letting them come in you?"

"No, huh-uh. Same like before. No humping. Don't matter to the johns neither. They just want to throw their coin away."

P waved to someone over Molly's shoulder.

"Look, Mol, you go back to the lid. I'll catch you there later. Tonight me and you and Wolf touch your father."

"Yeah, my father. You're more into that than into me."

"What do you mean? You're wrong, girl. This is special tonight. This coin's gonna get us the best in we ever got. And the coin from your father's gonna keep us in. That's how it's gonna be."

Molly backed away from him, turned, began to walk. But then she decided she wouldn't go to the lid. It was light, the city was up. She bought a newspaper and looked through it for some mention of the scam. But it was too soon. Tomorrow it would be in the papers for sure. On the tube. The front page was all about this new war in the Indian Ocean. Molly tossed the newspaper on top of a parked car. She was thinking whether she really wanted to go through with the scam at all, whether she wanted to be *in in in* all the damn time. P got her pissed, spreading for the johns—she didn't believe he wasn't humping—spreading his damn ass for the johns.

She was needing a boost. She had walked past South Artery where the homos were. Past Rad-Fill C where the radiation waste was dumped. Couldn't be more than 6:30. Traffic already heavy both ways on the Artery. She wiggled her ass, stopped, took out her compact, put on lipstick. Someone honked his horn. Youngish john in a big car. She motioned with her head, he turned down a utility road. Molly walked up to the car and got in. He started the car with his left hand, his right hand gripped her thigh.

Molly pushed his hand away.

"What do you want?"

He grinned. "Guess."

"No humping," she said.

"Why the hell not?"

"No humping, that's it."

He shrugged. "Blow-job then."

"Cost you fifty."

He looked her over with one eye. "You must be pretty stuck on yourself."

She shrugged. "That's the price."

He reached across her and opened the door. Stopping the car he pushed her out.

"Your lips are too thin," he shouted at her.

"Lousy shit!" she shouted at him, the diesel from his car in her face.

Traffic was heavy—she had a hard time getting off the Artery to the pedestrian strip. A short while later another john, sort of old-looking, pulled over. He paid thirty for a hand-job, then dropped Molly at Magda's lid.

Magda was inside alone, laying on her bed watching the tube.

"I need a boost," Molly said. "I got coin."

"In the drawer," Magda pointed. "Take what you need."

Molly used Magda's kit, gave herself a heavy jolt. In fact she felt a little like she was going to OD.

But it was okay. She got into the low wide bed with Magda and watched the tube. After a time she slept. When she woke the tube was still on and Magda was sleeping. Molly slept some more. When she awoke again Magda was standing naked, putting on her makeup. Molly had seen Magda naked before but had never noticed how tracked up her legs were, even her feet.

"How you feeling?" Magda said.

"Okay. Little dizzy."

Magda nodded.

"You gonna leave now?" Molly said.

"In a bit." Magda sat down on the bed. "Is it true what I heard?"

Molly looked at her.

"You and P gonna pull a scam?"

Molly nodded.

"Who came up with that? P?"

"P and Wolf," Molly said.

"Wolf? How'd he get a piece of this?"

Molly shrugged. "I guess P told him."

"Anything happen yet?" Magda said.

"What do you mean?"

"The scam start yet?"

"Yeah. P sent the kidnap letter to my father yesterday. Tonight him and Wolf are gonna phone my father, tell him where to leave the coin. Tell him some other stuff too."

"And Wolf is kinda helping P to keep the scam running slick, is that it?"

"I guess," Molly said.

"How much coin we talking about?"

"Five hundred thousand."

Magda just looked at her.

"What's the matter?" Molly said. "Don't you think it'll work?"

Magda shrugged. "Gotta go." She touched Molly's hair and left.

Molly got up and drank some cherry pop from the fridge. Her stomach felt lousy. She went into the toilet in the hall but it wasn't any good, she was as clogged as ever. She smoked one of Magda's cigarettes, then brushed her teeth with Magda's toothbrush. She went outside and was surprised how late it looked. Lots of wind too.

She walked for a while, taking the utility roads away from the Artery. Turning a corner she saw a crow land on the broken-up pavement, scrape with its beak at a dead blackbird that was stuck to the ground, then fly away with the remains in its talons. Suddenly another small blackbird was pursuing the crow real close, badgering it so that the crow had to perch on a ledge still with the dead bird in its claws. The blackbird perched close to it screaming at it. After a bit the crow took off and so did the blackbird flying above and below the larger bird, still on its ass. Flew out of sight.

Molly was walking to P's lid, but the wind was getting to her. She turned up to the Artery and got a cab, but then when they got to P's lid she saw she had no coin, must've left it on Magda's table. The cab driver wouldn't trust her to go into P's lid and get some coin and instead honked his horn for about ten minutes until Wolf came out. Wolf gave the driver coin and Molly went in with him to P's lid. P was laying on the bed real fucked-up.

"That was a mistake you just made, Molly," Wolf said.

She looked at him.

"By tonight your picture will be on the tube and in the papers and you just led that cabby right to where you were gonna hole up."

"Oh, I didn't think of that. Anyways, I don't think I want to go through with it—the scam."

Wolf laughed. "Too late now, girl. We already phoned your father. The drop is scheduled for tomorrow dawn. I'll put you up in my place."

"What's up with P?" she said.

"P's about to make it to the moon. Want some shit?"

"I guess."

"Later," Wolf said. "At my place."

Wolf pulled P out of bed and they went outside into Wolf's car. Wolf lived near West Artery in a regular flat, two rooms and a bathroom inside. He laid P down on the bed. P was still looking bad, like he almost OD'd or something.

Wolf said, "P'll pull out of it. He took too large a jolt. This shit's tasty. Let me cook you a dose."

Molly fixed. Wolf was right, it was good. Wolf always came up with tasty shit. Meanwhile P was pulling out. Molly laid on the bed next to him and they held hands.

Wolf turned on the tube and after a while they saw Molly on the screen, as well as a copy of the scam letter P had sent. Her father also came on speaking about how much he wanted her back, that the kidnappers shouldn't harm her, that they would get their money. Then Molly's mother came on, looking bushed as usual, saying she loved her daughter. Then some high cop came on saying the police would abide by her father's wishes and not try to ambush the kidnappers. That was it.

Wolf went out.

Molly helped P undress and they screwed. Then they laid in bed smoking cigarettes and drinking cherry pop. They kept the tube on without sound till they saw her picture flash on the screen. It was pretty much a repeat of the first thing they saw except in this one Molly's father and mother were together. Her father had his arm around her mother's shoulder. Molly felt her eyes fill—but then she giggled. So did P. It was the only time Molly had seen her parents touch since she was real small. In fact she didn't remember them touching then either, except she assumed they did.

The same high cop came on saying the same things as before. Then another cop without a uniform said some things about how they would not interfere with the kidnapping so as to ensure Molly's not getting killed and stuff.

They turned down the sound again.

Molly said, "I'd like us to get off shit for good."

"What do you mean?"

"With the scam money. Let's get off the shit and just go somewhere."

"Yeah," P said.

"Let's just go somewhere," Molly said. "Far away where we

could like . . . be away from this."

"Yeah," P said. Then: "Five hundred thou's a lot of coin. We'd never have to worry 'bout being low on shit."

"It ain't that great," Molly said. "Being in and stuff."

"Yeah, only what else is there? Who we gonna talk to?"

"What do you mean?" Molly said.

"We hardly know anybody who don't use. 'Cept Wolf."

"Yeah, Wolf," Molly said.

They laid on the bed and watched the tube.

"Where do you want to go?" P said.

"Huh?"

"When we get the coin? Where you want to go?"

"I don't know. Near the sea. I like water."

"The sea's fucked over," P said. "All those nuclear spills and shit."

"Not everywhere," Molly said. "It's not fucked over everywhere."

"I like mountains," P said.

"Right, we could go there. Mountains. Get a cabin."

P laughed.

"Why you laughing?"

"Ain't no more cabins," P said. "We'd have to get a condo. Which'd cost about what we're getting from the scam. Less what we give Wolf."

"How much we giving Wolf?"

"Hundred fifty thou."

"That much?"

"Yeah. He's into this almost as much as us."

"Whose idea was it in the first place?" Molly said. "Yours or Wolf's?"

"Kinda both. I guess his though."

"Magda was asking about it," Molly said. "The scam."

"Magda?"

"Yeah. I was with her when you were with the johns. Spreading for the johns." Molly pulled away from him.

P touched her head with his hand. "Don't get pissed with me. I couldn't let that coin go."

"Why not? We're about to get half a million. Ain't that enough?"

"Ain't never enough," P said. "Besides, what if it don't work?"

"You mean my father backing down?"

"Right. Or setting us up."

"That's what Fritz said," Molly said. "Fritz said something about it maybe not working."

"That's what I mean. This was supposed to be between me and you and Wolf. And now Fritz and Magda and who knows who else knows all about it. We shoulda been cool."

"You're scared," Molly said. "Why don't we drop it? There's time. I'll just show up at my mother's and say I was let go. That the kidnappers got scared and let me go."

"Too late," P said. "It's too late to drop it."

"You know something?" Molly said. "I'm scared too. This is the first time I'm like really feeling it."

"The shit's wearing off," P said. "Let's fix."

"It's kinda soon," Molly said. "Why don't we just stick some? Small boost."

"Small boost won't do me," P said, getting up. "Where the hell's your belt? Damn! It must be in my lid. Which ain't too damn smart. Not if the cabby leads the cops there."

"Just a sec," Molly said. "Wolf put a whole lot of stuff from your lid on the floor over there."

She got up and went to the corner of the small room. She held up the belt.

"Wolf's cool," P said.

"Someone got to be," Molly said.

P began to work on the shit.

"Not too much," Molly said. "You want to be clear for the scam."

"Scam ain't till dawn—six am."

"But you're gonna phone one more time, right? My father?"

"Wolf's doing it from outside. Phoning at ten. No, ten-thirty. I'll be okay by morning."

"Who's picking up the coin?"

"Me. Deal is soon's I have the coin and am out of sight, Wolf signals you to go on to Getty at East and Seminole. Where your father'll be. You'll be waiting for the signal at East and Pugh."

"Then what?"

P was cooking the shit.

"Then what, P?"

"Then we join up and spend the coin."

"What happens if my father . . . sends me away?"

"Like where?"

P had Molly's belt around his arm.

"Like nowhere," Molly said. She laid down on the bed on her stomach.

After he fixed P laid down next to her talking soft.

"We'll get together, Mol. Ain't no way we won't. Your old man makes the scam coin back in insurance. Plus he writes it off his taxes. He'll probably end up making more than he gave up. That's the way the shit works for the rich. How about a boost?"

"No."

"Little boost?"

"No—okay. Little."

Molly was going to just stick some, but she ended up using her belt for a fix.

"Guess what?" she said to P.

"What?"

"My birthday is Saturday. Just remembered."

"Hey," P said. "Sixteen, right?"

"Uh-huh."

"That's good. Your old man'll never let anything happen to you on your birthday."

"If he remembers."

"Did he last year?"

"I can't remember," Molly giggled.

She and P tried to screw but they were too fucked up. They smoked cigarettes, drank cherry pop and watched the tube. Every time the news came on there was something about the scam and Molly saw her face. It got to the point where it had nothing to do with her. Just the face of a thin girl with long brown hair. Daughter to an important-looking man with gray temples, and a wasted-looking woman who looked like the daughter but with wrinkles. There was also a lot of stuff on the new war in the Indian Ocean but Molly couldn't get what it was all about.

After a time she slept.

Someone was shaking the bed. Wolf, trying to get P up.

"Come on," Wolf said. "It's nearly ten. We have to phone the old man at quarter to eleven."

"I thought *you* were going to phone," Molly said.

"No," Wolf said. "P made the first contact, so it gotta be P."

"Where you phoning from?" Molly asked.

"Outside, couple of kilometers from here. Come on, P." Wolf shook him hard.

Finally P got up, Wolf got him dressed, and they left. Molly fell out again and for the first time in a long time she dreamed. Not the kind of dreams she had when she was in. A real dream. She remembered it when Wolf and P came back in slamming the door. *She is on the Artery walking barefoot against the traffic. All the cars and trucks are white and moving in the other direction. And then she isn't walking but sliding on her feet, first sort of medium speed, then fast, then out of control; the headlights don't see her, the cars somehow don't hit her. This changes: she is in a black steep tunnel still between the speeding cars and trucks and she is rolling—hurtling—down-grade over the rough surface, her arms and legs bruised and bleeding, shredding loose from her body. While all the headlights in the metal white bodies are speeding the other way. . .*

P stuck a lit cigarette in her lips.

"Done," he said.

"You phoned?"

"Right. He picked up on the first ring. No hassles. The coin'll be there at six. I even reminded him of your birthday."

"Yeah?"

"I said if you want Molly in one piece for her sweet-sixteenth don't fuck up."

"What he say?" Molly said.

"He said he'd play it straight." P looked at Wolf.

"If he drops the coin," Wolf said, "but the coin is marked, I know a party that'll pick it up and give us back two-thirds in unmarked. But I doubt it'll be marked."

"Yeah," P said.

Molly and P leave Wolf's lid at five-fifteen. (Wolf leaves later for Coolidge tower from where he sees the entire transaction.) P leaves Molly at East Artery and Pugh, then goes to Getty at East and Seminole. Soon as P cops the coin and is away free Wolf signals Molly with a white towel and she goes on to Getty and her father. Any kind of foul up and Wolf signals with a red towel, meaning Molly cuts out back to Wolf's lid. That's the deal.

Only what happens is P gets to the Getty drop on time and is ambushed, shot in the head and chest from close range with silencer .22s. This done, Wolf signals with his white towel and Molly goes on to Getty where she is snatched by the law. They take her to a lock-up downtown where her mother is waiting for her. Nothing passes between them. From the lock-up Molly is transported that same morning to the Rack, the detoxification center on Muscle Island.

With his needles, ink and two small brushes, the Tattoo Prince has completed yet another homemade. On the instep of his left foot: *a large animal with a single curved horn and heavy udders, its head bent as if trying to crop the grass.*

FIVE POEMS

JONATHAN GRIFFIN

RUSHING ABYSS

The seeing soul is fear
—a girl with her clothes on fire
We know the rushing abyss

Can faith defy this?

Inter-receding Heaven!
—from ever greater height
upwards the suns diving

apart to flawless night

FACING THE ANTIMUSIC

Forgive the new sin—
terracide in a sleep
heads that hide in the sand
of cities, to dodge how thin
the dust of stars how deep

Honor the brave who have ears
for the music of the spheres
—antimusic no breath
droning that death is death—
awake they hear it and live
on Earth in the Universe

minds   who still ask—brave
                having scanned
the many and far between

The age of faith is over:
ours has to be braver

TAKEN

Agnosticism—vow of poverty

Franciscans in Great Britain (my wife tells me)
        have this custom: often one
is sent out for six months into the world
        by himself—no money, only
                the clothes he's in

        no destination—God will guide him

They say it always works. For them it works

                        We are agnostics now:
                        to dare to see
                        is to take this vow
                        of poverty

                        Sight sends us out
                        alone with doubt:
        each of us—each time we dare—
        walks with nothing into what's there

There seems to be no God—
A Goddess in mortal danger is our guide

It works for us

For we are Hers
and there is grace
in this doomed Place

NOW THEREFORE IT MAY BE—

Grace versus God
the grace of Earth against a vandal God
Only the living Earth can
lift grace against God

Earth! grow in Man
the sap and leaves of grace
so this washed place
be birthplace of the salvation of God

Earth give us strength to hold grace out to God

EITHER . . . OR . . .

The self-blinding
a soul lying—
the sin against the light—
as if a poet lied

*

The span of listening—the silently
burning authority: woman or man
                    diffident,
                    awed wide
                                        when
          to hear could be to see
          and catch the unseen hand

NERO

JEREMY REED

Is it so terrible a thing to die?—
Exile's a termite to the intellect,
one's lines resound against an empty sky
on some craggy outpost where goats dissect
a clifftop for a mouthful. None are spared,
even the household gods have rubbled heads,
the shrine of Vesta's defiled, and thunder
rumbles its omens over every bed.
Two-headed offspring, lightning bolts, a snake
a woman gave birth to, still dribbling red,
its markings interfaced with jewels, predict
the impending whirlwind we live under,
scattering Rome's twenty-one district plots
into a smashed mosaic, in its wake
a cone of fire spins to avenge this spot.

Matricide stains his bad blood with worse blood.
Agrippina who curled upon her couch
enticing him to take her in a flood
of youthful frenzy, only had him touch
her pythonic hips through diaphonous
veils exposing her naked to her son.
He had her butchered, Britannicus too,
last of the Claudians, a brother done

to death, his gizzards shrivelled up in flame,
the whole deranged, effete imperial zoo
looking on, Burrus with his crippled hand,
Paris squawking, the eunuch retinue,
they buried him that night, even his name
was omitted from the ribald statue.

Men fear the streets at night; the city throbs
with Nero's bacchanalia, he ties
his victims up in bearskins, and the mob
assaults them, gobbing spit into their eyes.
If Poppaea rules his couch, she cannot stem
a lust for every perversion; he rules
by virtue of Seneca's diligence,
a man whose austere philosophic school
accrues to it more riches than the state.
I envy Suillius his penitence
and soft Balearic exile, no poet
can publish, the Emperor has preference
over Lucan, my pine enclaved estate
is eaten up by his indifference.

Our Empire cracks like worn crocodile skin,
it is a fishnet full of holes that flaps
at frontiers, Gauls, Frisians and Parthians
slough through the army's unprotected gaps.
Only in Britain does the eagle fly,
Suetonius licked a wild barbaric ruck
of troops marshalled by women—not a head
was saved—thousands stared from the horse-churned muck,
the smoking welter of a lashed rabble,
Boudicca's skin booted the blue of lead,
and yet that country's an untamed thicket,
its forests resist our tapemeasure roads.
Today our drill's the anemic babble
of men who sit squat as paunch-bellied toads.

The model ivory chariots on his board
are playthings like the laurel that he wears

to face his golden statue with its bored
expression. Twenty times his height it stares
towards the ceiling's fretted ivory.
The tyrant in The Golden House who sweats
beneath the lead weights placed upon his chest
for better respiration to abet
his vocal chords. His husky voice can't range
to the empyrean, and when he rests
he wears a robe constellated with stars.
Rome's become an international exchange
for gladiators, charioteers, mock wars,
there's not a statue's head that doesn't change.

His eye's his mirror, not a mirror stares
from the imperial rooms, in case she shows,
the dead mother who drags him by the hair
from sleep and suffocates him by a slow
immersion in an ant hill. Nothing quells
the raging insomnia that has him run
tilting at statues, the amphitryon
of ransacked Greek gods, naked in the sun
that finds him rocking the gold statuette
of Victory, placed by the horn of Ammon;
the Red Sea's dredged for pearls to spot his room.
whoever marries him must thread the net
of red and purple he throws at the moon,
Octavia died, a blade in her gullet.

The fire that gutted Rome, fanned by a wind
that stoked the blaze to a red tidal wave,
was at his instigation. In their minds
men have already placed him in a grave
dogs foul with their stench. Things are upside down,
gold sand for wrestlers comes in place of wheat,
naumachias demand monsters from the deep,
to be salvaged by a carnival fleet,
Africa and India's scoured for beasts,
smashed up like firewood—the Emperor can't sleep,
so must be entertained until the sand

in the arena's troughed with blood. He feasts
on peacocks encased in gold leaf, and stands,
divine exemplar of the human beast.

Profanation of every rite decrees
an inauspicious death. Men swallow words
like stones; each week a new conspiracy's
unearthed, the plotters are killed first then heard,
their heads are packed into an apple bin,
even Seneca's had to renounce life,
his riches the Emperor's gratuity.
In Rome it doesn't pay to be a wife
who mourns a husband for she joins his pyre:
our only common law is treachery.
Paranoid, flanked by Mazacian horsemen,
nibbling aphrodisiacs to refire
his spent member, the songbird in his den
thinks only of night. Lust heats like a wire.

Tyrant follows tyrant on thinning ice,
and each at last plunges to the black pool
to solidify. New taxes, new vice,
supersede before the old corpse can cool.
Nero deserted by the army ran
to some outlying villa, unprepared
for death, dusty, his silk clothes burred with thorns,
his unskilled sword hand trembling and his scared
eyes appealing for respite. It took two
hands to assist him with the knife, his torn
windpipe gouting blood. The mob would have flayed
him alive, or thrown him inside a sack
into the Tiber. Now Galba's arrayed
in purple, men wish the old tyrant back.

Height: average, rarely used to good effect,
the body pustular, pitted with sores,
the features unpronounced as a defect,
but epicene, profuse sweat in the pores.
The eyes sea blue, prone to be myopic,

the neck squat on a pepperpot torso,
the belly already protuberant,
the legs spindly, hair dyed, the voice a slow
drawl quickly mounting to hysterical
passion, the eyes made up in indigo.
Histrionic, his one pursuit pleasure,
facetious, inordinately jealous,
hellbent, I itemize his faults to cure
the harsh exile of one Sosianus.

FIRES FROM CHAGALL & DREAMING CLOUDS WITH KLEE

RIEMKE ENSING

making a poem / for my father

Signs and patterns are what is common.
That line might be a flock of birds
migrating, could be the first stroke
towards saying I've changed   my mind
not liking trickery, the games we play
the line we draw elaborately across
time   forgetting the magic of color and the sun
going down red   over the horizon
in one fell swoop being swept off
the edge of the world and you're left
completely in the dark as to where
you are going.

A painter might draw beside you
symbols of landscape   recognizably centered
as cloud in the window of the neighbor's
house / not moving though the wind blows.
A tree perhaps to shape you by / its leaves
making any one of four seasons.
These signs we decipher. They tell

stories ripe as aubergine or persimmon,
tall as any dictionary where treasure is
kept.

persimmon, n. diospyros kaki.
American date plum
yellow fruit becoming
sweet when softened
by frost / persimmon
native of China bright
fruits will hang on
the tree in winter /
persimmon deciduous
small native to Japan
can be in weeping
form attractive both
in leaf and fruit
after leaves have
fallen / persimmon
dios divine.

So much for words lying
their way from one book to another
way of saying here are the words they tell
me a thing or two mostly
they are not the sound I want /
to hear the wind
in branches the sun orange lush
or persimmon / dios, divine
the words has its limits
go and see the tree
put the fruit in your hand, your mouth,
mix shape and form with what
you feel and see and mostly touch
and smell or taste and hear.

Let the poet draw circles
round the moon / the painter till
his garden plant trees for us

to sit under and smile
as the wind does when it's up
to mischief and blows human flowers
into the book we could be.

These words are about lines scored
with burin or pen / how charcoal spirits
away the harsh imprint of winter engraved
needle sharp on the mind like poems,
the lithographs of sound shaped
by a point fine as glass drawing
blood from the stained window
of the heart shaped as magic flame dressed
gayer than harlequin riding on rooster
or peacocks reaching for rainbows.

In the line you draw
such notions grow   that we hear
the hiss of the sun as he kisses
the water good night / and what is
known   might go in any direction
of loss   where legends take root
and roads become symbols
of danger   closed in winter
and red as impossible escape.

Past is place and shape.
A house in a street with a square
of grass where you might see
the sky falling   between walls
standing like trees touching
each other with darkness.

The search is always for the other
side of whatever it might be
you're looking for in skies that brood
in all that detail of frown   and restless
waves   you fared on   at the edge of winter
when salt lines drew naked wind straight
from the sea scarring this shore.

Autumn might have been
as simple as a Cézanne fruit
garden, but we were miles away
across oceans   migrating.

I say nothing
of childhood when everything is
clear   and lines belong
to burnt-ochre faces in portraits
that might smile
as if the moon had passed
through the street like a shadow.

Night comes tied up in black
columns of death / notices
under the arm of the evening star
that you died this morning.

Winter falls in summer   this year

I go in to bury my father.

He is not a man
I recognize other than
images I have seen
before / his eyes are closed.

The picture is described.
The grey more sad than any pencil
mark can make on paper through a room
of color / touching even white
and death.

All these are fragments of meaning.

Father, I should have touched you /
met whatever region of warmth was
in the colors you were before
the ice crept into the walls
of the timid room.

This image I fear will remain
a dream / but it is far
from ending / there already
I see
the beginning.

Photographs are left in drawers.

You do not know me   but I am
not / a stranger to you.

The light has gone from the lamp.
Under the tree the talking
has vanished and singing
is motionless in clouds
where the knife is raised
blood red and sighing.

These pictures are the smell of a poem hung
up to dry like linen in the damp night
when sounds might break through the window
into that space   where suddenly
a tear is the music stars make
in the calligraphy of trees
and our sighs / rise on patterns
of rhyme with the wind
in bright pennants dancing
through flames of grass.

All this I shore up / make
pieces of colored paper with
to toss up to the sky like a flight
of so many colored dragonflies
or the beautiful bird listening
to music starred with poems
serried as notes frail on a complex stave
of lines coming
together as tiny rainbows.

The idea is to contain a world
in the strokes the pen makes across
paper / the line you read / between
the words which might be there
or could be simply other
than expected.

A sequence of events signalling
danger / a network to decode
and songs for a death coming
suddenly clearly among sirens
wailing in a street full
of movement and light / shades
of bizarre mimes making
pastiches for writers.

The words speak for themselves
but the color is personal / somber
or black   depending on the gesture;
the way the earth might burn orange
or bitter as the lemon tree
very pretty and small in yellow days
when houses fall.

What matters is a sense / of order.
The table under the colored window,
the rattan blind down against sun,
the mat on the floor facing
Mecca where such colors might come
from rocks and sand blowing
through bleached grass and the tree
of life / firm
and reaching to the mihrab
where the holy city
lies.

The poem I started is already
lost.   One day I will find it
on a sheet of paper pulled out

from a pile of books or unanswered letters.
Perhaps it will be
a bookmark showing the way
to mushroom growing or porcelain
glazes delicate as the smudge of Puzzuoli
red in a sketch where nothing is
sentimental but all lives to speak
clearly as words do when they cry
from the heart without design
or drama / plainly as a flight of birds caught
in the sharp magic of black surprising
with its coat of colors.

EVERYONE KNOWS SOMEBODY WHO'S DEAD

B. S. JOHNSON

So you like the title? That is the first thing, they say here, the *Title.*

Conflict, they say, as well. I should engage my reader in a *Conflict.*

That is easy. What I have in mind is the conflict between understanding and what does not appear to be understandable. Few subjects could be more interesting. Surely you must see that? I trust you, not knowing you.

It is also the partialness in the *Soul* (not a word I have ever used before, I think) *of Conflict* that concerns me here.

There is *Resolution* at the end, I see, skipping ahead. Be calm. I have written before. Trust me, not knowing me.

This is the difference between doing it and teaching it. Perhaps. Who am I to presume? I am (like you) everyone to presume, there is no one else.

Conflict, it says here. *Of three kinds, viz.: within the self; without the self, with other humans; without the self, with nonhuman forces.* Gross simplification, but what else is there?

One conflict is within me, certainly. Many, rather. But what I have to write of is not a conflict within him: indeed it is rather of that moment of perfect nonconflict, in the end, of unity, unison, when his self was absolutely at one with his nonself, when the will and the act itself were in accord, at peace, were the same.

One should also start at the *Beginning,* it says here. That I could have done, easily.

I first met him at the evening college of London University, Birkbeck College. We must have sat next to one another at some lecture or another. English and Latin were what we had in common, History and I think Economics were points of divergence. Everyone had to do Latin. He was tall, angular is unfortunately the only word, smart: I was none of these. He introduced me to the *New Statesman* and his fiancée, a dumpy, curly blonde quite unlike him in almost everything, unsuited, I thought. Or perhaps think now, with hindsight. I introduced him to me, I was all I had. We joined the college rowing club together, Saturday afternoons for that Spring we would imagine the exercise did us good. I may still have a key to their locker half a generation later, they may still have in it my heavy white wool sweater. He worked in an office quite near mine, both in Kingsway. Occasionally we would meet for lunch, too. Shell was his company, Standard-Vacuum mine, oil was another thing we had coincidentally in common. His job I cannot remember, mine is . . . *Irrelevant.*

A Plot is. . . .

There were other things. Bengs and Joyce were also friends, at this time. We each passed our examinations. He and I went separate ways, then. We left Birkbeck, the evening lectures and steady jobs, both managed to become possessed of grants to go full-time to different colleges, though still of London University. I chose mine because I thought well of the name, he his because he admired the staff. We were both five years mature. The Registrar warned me, objecting to my full-time going, that I at twenty-three would be amongst a lot of eighteen-year-old girls. That is probably also amongst the things which are not relevant.

. . . a Conflictful Situation. . . .

There was a party for Birkbeck friends, he and I met the curls at the Albert Hall (built as a rendezvous), the rain was heavy in a way not common in July. Probably that summer too I went once and never again to the family home, Churchill Gardens, tall flats aligned north and south so that the sun set garishly on the supper table. The conversation centered, so I remember, Bengs was there, on the way the place was warmed by surplus heat generated across the river at mighty Battersea power station, piped presumably. They were very early postwar reconstruction or development.

. . . Exacerbated by Additional Circumstances of Increasing Difficulty. . . .

He bought an identifying scarf for his new college. I obtusely wanted nothing of such symbols, it was more than enough that I was admitted. Though they looked warm, and the winter might be coming.

That summer also I was best man at his wedding to the unlikely curls. I was brought in late, a kind of locum, second best man. I do not know why the first choice man was not available. I did wonder then and later that he should have so few friends that I, little more than an acquaintance, and recent, too, should be honored. But that is speculation. I am allowed a little speculation?

. . . Proceeding to one or more Abortive Efforts to overcome the Situation.

The marriage was at a church overlooking Brighton. The spire was said to be a blessing to mariners, as well.

It was a modern church. I produced the ring without any of the mishaps celebrated in tradition. Afterwards in the vestry, is it called, I paid the gentleman vicar. He kept what the other functionaries were owed and pressed back on me his own share, saying, It is something I do for young couples, I love weddings, you see. You see.

At the reception I stole an epigram from Oscar Wilde, something about a spade. My punishment was that it fell flatter than a discus. And they probably thought I was bent, too, all those relatives, to boot. This occasion represents my only appearance as a best man. At another wedding, where the best man's name was Fat Gerald, the bride's father asked me to make a speech because I was a writer and writers were good at speeches. But one of the reasons I am a writer is because I am no giver of speeches at weddings or anywhere else, I explained to him. I do not think he understood, he remained disappointed.

You would not be forgiven for thinking my life one long round of weddings, the like.

The first (or Oscar) wedding reception was at a hotel on the front. Very pleasurable, being at the seaside with something proper to do, with a purpose, and with friends, like Bengs, in this case. But the epigram, and reading the telegrams, too, were almost distressing. And so was the bill. My duties as best (available) man it seems, included paying for the reception. Not out of my own money, the father of the bride footed. I cast the bill carefully and quickly, being at that time more an accounts clerk than a student. It seemed the least I could do following the pagan flatness of my speech. Mine was nothing approximate to the maître's total, differing by some fourteen pounds if I remember as accurately as I cast. A considerable sum, even more considerable (as ever) then. The difference was in the favor of the maître, no surprise, or of those who employed him. His apologies were certainly profuse, though practiced and just not concealing a challenge to my sharpness. The bride's father was noticeably grateful to me. The maître must have hoped we were all too drunk by then. Perhaps more often than not that is the usual state at the end of these functions. I hardly remember the bride and groom during this wedding: only her on the church path after, him in the church as we awaited the delegation. Perhaps that is as it should have been.

Abortive is shortly a good word in context.

Three years for our respective degrees, ha, and we hardly saw each other. One occasion though I remember with some clearness:

a Fireworks Day, one of three, by deduction. A dinner or supper with him and the curls, me and my moll, what a metonym. The streets, afterwards, of Pimlico—("Have at thee, then, my merrie boyes and hey for old Ben Pimlicos nut browne"—as it occurs first written down in News from Hogsdon, 1598. But no doubt they would frown on such a scholium as having no place.). There were fireworks in the streets, we threw them, a bonfire on a bombsite, St. George's something the road was called, in Pimlico, where one may be catered for but hardly satisfied.

Then when we had both just finished we met in the coffee bar in Malet Street next to Dillons, on purpose. We were able to tell each other what we had done in between. The marriage was just become or becoming a divorce. My moll had cast me off in favor of a sterile epileptic of variable temperament. But yes! Now I remember exactly, ha! We had not just finished, but were finishing, finals. One of the days we met in the Rooms, I feel they called them, arranged to meet afterwards downstairs. And thence to the coffee bar. On our way, talking at a junction, waiting, just before Euston Road, to the south, I could look it up, gazetteers are to hand, but why should I? Am I not allowed to be lazy too? Or reckless? But as we stood talking at this junction, she who was once my moll appeared in the long distance, walked the long way towards us, crossed the other wide diagonal, went the long way away. And all that while I tried to talk as though I were unaware of her, of all that she had meant to me, of all those things I have exorcised elsewhere. Ah.

After the coffee we made an evening of it, did the thing most opposite to degree finals we could think of at such notice: front row of the royal circle at the Victoria Palace. The Crazy Gang were then tailing off, we could have sat anywhere, at any price, they would have had us. No doubt there were other funny things, we were raucous with relief, but now I remember only a game they played with a fat lady, throwing old pennies so they landed flatly on her bare mottled old chest, briefly, then dropped into her cleavage. There were things like that, then. No doubt we also caught up then, though since I was without any direction, where was he?

Robin (now I have to name him) had taken up with a student, a girl in the year below him (before, during or after the divorce was unclear), a Swiss who was having an affair also with a much older man with money, and all that went with it, a car. The curls, he told me, had had an abortion, arranged with confounding liberality (for this was in what was thought of as the heyday of the back-street abortionist) by his tutor, to whom he had gone for help in this matter. The marriage was virtually broken, after less than a year, and satisfaction at having foreseen their short incompatibility was not absent from my remarks at the death on this occasion. But I could not have acted otherwise, in marrying her, I am sure, emotionally, he insisted. But there had been hints, heard over the telephone not long before Finals, that they had parted. I was put off, easily, working all that afternoon by indecision as to ringing her and attempting to take sexual advantage of the state she might or might not have been in. I did not know about the heyday then, and after all I had been more or less best man.

It occurs to me now because of this and other things that I could not and cannot call myself his friend. Was he capable of friendship? I do not think so. Am I? It was more a working relationship, he was like a colleague though we had no common enterprise or ambition beyond both being working-class boys bent on an education, the illusion that that was the key to—

Extension is always achieved by the Insertion of one or more Abortive Efforts.

There was another occasion. Bengs and I went to a Wandsworth hill road, in the curls' time. Of more I have no recollection.

Their *Comprehensive Scheme* should deal with this *Common Problem.* But it does not.

It was another flat in which I remember him next, as it may be, in Old Brompton Road, the corner of Drayton Gardens, near the powerhouse of the literary trade union movement. Though I was then of course unaware of its militancy. And now I am quaintly aware of one of those loops in time where. . . . but you do not need me to explain that cliché of the twenties. What has happened is more important, of certain interest to me, and what has happened is that I have remembered that the girl I took to this Old Brompton Road flat Robin had was in fact the very same girl whose marriage I attended all those years later and whose father I disappointed! This can be no coincidence: a real loop in time has happened. I think I did not want to marry her myself. I was at that time between girls I wanted to marry. But it is a curious loop, though I have not wanted for more curious. And while describing it the one thing I remember is that we four (the Swiss being there too) discussed a topical tragedy in the world of politics, Sharpeville. The reason I remember what he said is that he was shortly proved to be right: in that the Sharpeville massacre, far from being the spark which would ignite a conflagration to consume the old repressive system, was on the contrary more likely to be the flame which would harden into steel the iron resolve of the oppressors. I do not know that his imagery was as elegantly contrived as mine is, but he had written an unpublished article about the incident, for (I think) a serious weekly. But he was remarkably right! I am myself never right for anyone else but me, and not too often do I achieve that small victory. How many times have you yourself been right for other people, then? Ah.

He was at this time teaching at some South London secondary school, his writing was towards another job. If ever you want to make a lot of money, he told me, open a sweetshop next to a school, the kids are in and out all day long. As we left I told the Swiss privately I thought that what he had read to us of his writing had . . . saleability! As though I knew, it was mere politeness!

The Solution Stage. . . .

Perhaps it was this perceptive rightness which led him inevitably to a post on the *Evening Standard* at the City Desk.

. . . involves the character in
either (a) overcoming his problems . . .

How full everyone's life is! Why, I hardly knew him and here I am well past two thousands words already!

. . . *or (b) succumbing to them.*

Later in this stage they visited me. I cannot avoid the thought that he was showing me that he had arrived in the world of affairs before I had. That is, he had a car and after eating curry out he bought a whole bottle of whisky to take back to the flat I had then. I think he even told me how much he was earning; it seemed at that time I was managing adequately on about a quarter of his salary. I think he wanted not only to show me he was doing well but that his way of doing well was better than mine. My way then was simply to try to write as well as those exemplars from the past I had chosen to set up whilst at college. Neither did it escape my notice that he was ahead in the matter of a mistress, too, and a glamorous foreigner at that. All I had to show was a bound set of page proofs of my first novel: high hopes as I had of it, I do not remember it as being sufficient to set against the car, the whisky, and the Swiss mistress.

What other news from Hoxton?

A finished copy before publication I took around to dinner at their flat, still in Pimlico, some (presumably short) while later. I do not remember what Robin said about the book on this occasion: at some time previously he had expressed great scepticism about what it was trying to do. He was right if the amount of money garnered was his criterion. Perhaps it was; or was not. Present was a very pleasant, charming and witty man of about our age called Charles, who was by way of being a printer and an actor, though not necessarily in that order. I think Robin had meanwhile made a daring leap from the *Standard* to a young, vital organ which was highly relevant and called *Topic.* Robin became either its business manager or writer on business affairs, business editor: I think the latter. Much talk of a world I did not know, very high-powered, men who were coming or all the go at the time, have since gone even further, some of them, his colleagues in print.

Have I finished with the *Abortive Effort(s)* yet?

I have recently become aware that an uncomfortable number of my contemporaries are dying before what I had imagined to be their times, simply jacking it all in, for one reason or another.

There was another, hardly remembered. The landlady of a friend with the same forename as myself. Her daughter came up to attend to the disposition of the remains and remnants. She was married to a naval officer, the daughter. My friend made (he convinced me) steamy love with her, unexpectedly, in some sort of consolatory reaction to the mother's death. She had drunk a bottle of gin and sealed the drawing room cracks and turned the gas on. Probably for her a comfortable, euphoric occasion, making herself comfy: I imagine her not desperate. The day after, the daughter and my friend were alone in the house, the naval officer as if nowhere. She had to stay the night, it was only nature, my friend was sure. My friend was also a colleague at work in a sweet factory, and he was remarkable amongst my acquaintance in that each morning after an evening on the beer he would wake up to find the plimsols he used as slippers seeping with urine. It could clearly be no one else's but his own, though at the same time he could never remember having risen in the night to perform. He would relate each occasion to me, baffled, whenever we . . . but I digress, and the *XLCR Plotfinder* leaves me unclear as to whether digressions are permitted.

Oh, I look forward to my own deathbed scene: the thing I shall have to say which I could not say before!

The *Topic* job was a great success but the magazine collapsed, ahead of its time in some respects, I seem to remember. Robin went (though there may have been a hiatus) back to the *Standard* as full-blown City Editor. We were proud of him, Bengs and I, and others, too.

I meant to tear it out, I was in a foreign country, I never did.

My wife and I, newly married, visited Robin and the Swiss girl, Vivienne, something like as newly married, now, I think, at their new small house in Maida Vale, very demure, bijou. We had a meal, supper or dinner as usual. He showed me the room that he intended to fill with his files. A comprehensive filing system, he informed me, was a major factor in the success of any journalist: one simply collected facts together from many sources, filed them under subjects, and regurgitated them in new combinations as one's own articles.

Soon we must arrive at the *Resolution* or *Point of Solution*. . . .

Not long afterwards we took him up on the offer of the gift of a large wardrobe he had made himself from battens and hardboard, collected it in the old navy blue banger of a van which was the first four-wheeled vehicle I had ever owned. He described how the wardrobe was the first thing he had made for the home in the palmy days of the curls, how it was constructed over-elaborately and uneconomically due to his lack of craftsmanlike experience. He had, unexpectedly and soon, an opportunity to demonstrate its methods of construction since it became stuck on the third flight of stairs up to our second-floor flat and we had to take it to pieces there to move it any higher. They had decently followed us in their car, a bigger car, and helped us carry the wardrobe. But there we were, unsocially stuck, we above having access to our flat, they below; it was hardly possible to pass even refreshments between. I have taken it to pieces myself since then, on moving out five years later. I reassembled it for lodgers, and then on another advent I had it in bits again, roughly, crudely, with the children. It had served us well, I burnt it in the yard. Except for one piece I shall keep, have before me for this piece, having cut a foot specially with his writing on it, in pencil, curious things that confirm how he said he made it: OSSPIECE, it says, cut off by the removal necessary for a tee-halving joint, TOP BACK. Yes, the point is in. SCREW TOP ONTO X1 PIECE. IT WILL HAVE TO BE SHORTENED BY TWICE THE WIDTH OF THIS. What writing! It was always rickety, was unsightly from the first, too, we accepted it only because we had no money for a proper one.

. . . *which can admit of a Surprise Ending.*

Mostly professional things. They must have visited us in that flat when we had straightened it; I was very careful about reciprocating hospitality in those days. We learnt at one point he had been demoted to Assistant through the return of a former City Editor, a star; this was an uncomfortable arrangement but we understood he accepted it. Not so very much later he was promoted again when the star ascended ever higher. One anecdote he told us concerned traveling in a taxi with the super star and Vivienne: a carefree cyclist overtook them, dodging in and out, glorying in his mobility amongst the impacted cars in Regent Street, until some minutes later near the Vigo Street junction he was involved in a jam of his own causing which he was unable to avoid since his brain was now distributed hither and thither.

All that time, and the only exact words of his I remember are some of those spoken in the Malet Street coffee bar on that one occasion: "Life is a series of clichés, each more banal than the last."

I certainly do not feel up to inventing dialogue for your sake, going into oratio recta and all that would mean. These reconstructed things can never be managed exactly right, anyway. I suppose I could curry a dialogue in which Robin and I argued the rights and wrongs of his *Conflictful Situation,* but it would be only me arguing with myself: which would be even more absurd than trying to write of someone else's life.

The last I think I saw of him was at the home of a smart lawyer to whom I had originally introduced him. I remember feeling resentful that they now knew each other better than I knew either of them. We have diverged, I thought, arrogantly, geometrical progression cannot be unwelcome.

It must have been perhaps two years later that I attended some quiet function and met again the charming Charles. He said he was very relieved to be able to tell me that our mutual friend Robin appeared to have sorted himself out at last, after his trouble. I had not heard of any trouble, I told him apologetically. With genuine sorrow, Charles explained that Robin had become involved with another girl and Vivienne had as a result successfully gassed herself. I was equally genuinely shocked, and guilty, too, that I had not been in touch with him for the period within which this had happened. Then I shared his relief that Robin had recovered to the extent that he was living with another girl: whether this was the same another girl I do not remember Charles telling me. No doubt I could find out by ringing him now and perhaps inviting him round for one of supper, dinner, or a drink.

Patience: we are about to reach the *Solution Point.*

I was for three months in Paris at the time, and nervously keeping in touch by purchasing the airmail edition of *The Times* perhaps every third day. Thus I was again genuinely shocked to read of his death only by a one-in-three chance. I cannot at this stage remember if I read a news story and the obituary, or only the latter. I seem to know that he too employed the good offices of the North Thames Gas Board, but whether this was from the newspaper or later from the splendid Charles, or some other source, I cannot ascertain. I meant to tear it out, the way one does, and never does. It cannot happen with North Sea Gas, I am assured. But certainly I read the obituary, which was without a photograph, I think. It was not very long. After some facts, the only opinion expressed as to how he might be remembered, or had been in any way remarkable, concerned the way in which he had helped to find out what was in the minds of businessmen by organizing a luncheon club at which they were invited to meet the press. There was more than that, but that is all it said, all there was to say, his life summed up, the obituary, full point.

There. I have fully satisfied the XLCR rules, I think. Popular acclaim must surely follow.

GREEKLY GONE

JAMES L. WEIL

In memoriam, Aleksis Rannit

Olumpos
piped the six

notes the six
windbells blow

kisses make
six hundred

songs love each
other so

Aleksis
Greekly gone.

FOUR POEMS

JAAN KAPLINSKI

Translated from the Estonian by the author and Sam Hamill

EVERY DYING MAN

Every dying man
is a child:
in trenches, in bed, on a throne, at a loom,
we are tiny and helpless
when black velvet bows our eyes
and the letters slide from the pages.
Earth lets nobody loose: it all
has to be given back—breath, eyes, memory.
We are children when the earth
turns with us through the night toward morning
where there are no voices, no ears, no light, no door,
only darkness and movement
in the soil and its thousands
of mouths, chins, jaws, and limbs
dividing everything so that
no names and no thoughts remain
in the one who is silent lying in the dark
on his right side, head upon knees.
Beside him, his spear, his knife,
and his bracelet, and a broken pot.

VERCINGETORIX SAID

Vercingetorix said: Caesar, you can take
the land where we live away from us,
but you cannot take the land from us where we have died.

I've thrown down my sword at your feet.
That is how we are, my people and I;
I know what is coming.
All those who deserved to live
in the Arvernian land are dead,
and I do not want to live
with those who are left.

I know they will, I can see them
learning the tongue of the masters, forgetting their fathers' speech.
I see them shamed by their eyes' blueness,
by their elders and their uncouth talk,
I see them as Romans clutching the papers of citizenship to their
breasts.

So be it, Imperator. Let there be one language
in your republic, one faith and one people,
let the road be secure and smooth
for your soldiers, merchants, and thieves
as far as Ultima Thule
and up to the River Styx.

I shall be flogged to death on the Capitol
but my love and my anger
cannot be put to death.
My anger will remain alive
to shout like an owl in the hollow years.
Destruction to you and to your insatiable city,
Caesar!
Revenge will rise up like an oak
from the acorn of your desires.

Your state will come and go.
Wheat will grow on your squares, and goats will graze on your
Forum.
It is my hand and the hand of my people
that will bring you down,
my hand wielding the sword of the Vandals.

The hour will arrive when Roman pride
will not bend a single blade of grass beside the Roman road,
the hour will arrive when the gluttonous city
will burst like a leech beneath the fists of those
who come from the East and the South and the North.

Do what you want and will:
I know sword and club await me
because all who deserved to live
in the Arvernian land are dead.

IF YOU WANT TO GO

If you want to go
do not remain if only for our sake
because we do not understand—thirty years
forty years of thirst of sunsets and sunrises in dusty windows
who then can say whither and how long yet
who then will answer us if you
take your hand
from your mother's hand
from your father's hand
and the wind takes your hand and you go

on aspen leaves
the tiny feet of the sun walk
into evening
today always and for a long time yet

we are given too much and we are
very poor
we are taught too much and we know
nothing

> but we too we do not want
> to inhabit the same world
> as an Oliver Cromwell or a Jossif Stalin

but we must remain—wagons
athwart, sideways on the road
we have no speech and no voice if you go
look back once more wait

> fields are fanning green scarves
> meadows are fanning motley scarves
> you are melting away between grass and bumblebees

the road rises and descends again
you go and will not return—the hands of a windmill
are waving when you are already on the other side of the hill
when we all are we all will be

> everyday life hair grows even after death
> free time motorcycles catalepsy
> paraplegy anabiosis crimes and punishments

we shall all be free we shall see
what it really is it will anyway have an end
and we have enough time do not go before us wait
some time some mile on the king's dismal plain
in the land of burnt tanks and turning wheels
because we must find the way

> long sandy straight openings
> to put your head on the naked knees of the forest
> and sleep until the end

when you forget us and smile to the windmill on the hillside
and go away who will help us

to the gate and say to them there
that we are back

white rivers are lost in white sand
yellow rivers are lost in yellow sand
in the blue eyes of my child
the land beyond forests shines

home shelter courtyard well
rooster's crow opening buds
all awake with all all together with all

but nothing is ready yet
nothing will ever be ready
in the long dreams of the children
is God himself dreaming of his dreams

the windmill is playing with wind the road rises and descends again
do not go yet remain
remain with us for we do not yet know a thing

a red cloud cuts the sun into halves
the sky is full of martlets

IF I WANTED TO GO BACK

If I wanted to go back
I should know that the thoughts
I thought going through the empty houses
are as empty as the houses
where moths gnaw and fungus eats
the walls and where the spinning wheel stands alone
in the corner, where the spade stands alone
before the threshold. This emptiness is great indeed,
as is the land. Each one is someone else

from everywhere and leads the way
somewhere else, and no one could ever
walk through all this land:
every beginning is different after its end
than it was before it ended, and everything is always
something else: the houses remain empty
and I haven't the strength, nobody has the strength
to live and die with everyone,
to step across your thresholds, sleep in all your beds.
My abandoned land, lifeless land, how
I try to tear myself away from you, how
can I be and live with all these new things
that have no face or manner? Thus, I put
my hand against the moth-eaten beam
and get up and go: the darkness lies equally on everything and everyone,
the darkness is large enough for our land and for all of us.

FIVE POEMS

JUANA ROSA PITA

Translated from the Spanish by Donald D. Walsh

THE HEIGHT OF LETTERS

Poetry is written by hope
and desire subscribes it between the lines:
the letter that results
                                        from the irrational rite
of filling inkwells with blood
and opening experience by its whitest face
setting it on the table
under the moistened fire

Poetry is the unreasonable letter
openly registered and addressed to everybody
with nobody's address:
                                    intended for tomorrow
the only letter that we consider lost
if it just reaches somebody

Poetry is the height of letters:
                                        inside are the powers
destined by love
for endless communion

LETTER TO MY ISLAND

Island
far from you is near the most
sensitive point
in the wound of time:
far from you my flowing body
on a bed of edges
that threaten the wind

Far from you thirst and hunger
are not quenched
with flattery of fruit and streams of water:
far from you is the solid solitude
(those who live in you know only
the other solitude:
the one that has eight letters):
                    island
far from you is inside the empty
well of dreams

Far from you my hands run
eagerly
over the flesh of a world of poetry:
even pain
                    even pleasure
shift in me
through an abstract moan at the edge of the earth

Island
far from you my life is irony
the tender scrawl of an absent writer:
a straw
in the sky's symbolic eye

CONFIDENTIAL LETTER TO ANOTHER POET

This word
that jumps from my pen
beginning the unexpected parade
toward who knows where:
this word that wants to be
memorable bread
being the daughter of hunger and thirst
and spreads its letters over the page
like a newborn
on a loving blanket:
this mendicant word
love it;
let yourself fall with your eyes shut
inside it
as if you did not exist
like one who wants to give
the mortal sword thrust to pronouns
like one who can
display against the light
a chaliced territory:
this word shouting
that you don't understand
for it has no time here
but that you can inhabit naked
now
like a sun-filled room
if you blot yourself out
inadvertently:
this unpronounceable word
like a sad window
is the luminous region where dwells
the most atrocious
desolation

FINAL LETTER OF REPORT

La vie comme un passeport vièrge
—André Breton

Every day I die of existence
and wrapped in the shroud of my name
I am unfaithful to life

I love therefore I am
I say again
but I love with measure
and like everyone I shall die
of fatal indifference at some moment

Unless my being loses all restraint
and is displaced
by way of love
like a ray of light toward the others

ILL TIMED

It is time of roots
like white handkerchiefs
it is a time to go from sun to tears
embracing
the orphan figure of men:
exiled from heaven
(from a foamy isle)
exiled from the other
(from a shoreless love)
exiled from being
(from an open brotherhood)
still
exiled from the dream

FOUR POEMS

LÊDO IVO

Translated from the Brazilian Portuguese by Giovanni Pontiero

THE DESTROYER

Love is not an architect.
Like the termites, it destroys
the most solid construction
from walls to roof.

Defending the indefensible,
love has no respect for intellect.
Like a mouse, it comes out and nibbles
the abstract bread and the concrete sun.

Love? Two plus two do not make four.
The right path in the wrong cavity,
something twisted in a straight mattress.

Love! successive hills,
obelisk, a devouring tongue,
a question put to the Holy Ghost!

THE GATE

My gate stays open all day long
and is closed by me at night.
I expect no nocturnal visitors
save for the thief who leaps over the wall of dreams.
The night's deep silence draws me to listen
to nascent fountains in the forests.
My bed, white as the Milky Way
confines me in the darkness of night.
I occupy the world's entire space. My careless hand
topples a star and startles a bat.
The beating of my heart intrigues the owls
among the cedar trees as they ponder the enigma
of day and night delivered by the waters.
In my petrified dream I remain still yet travel.
I am the wind that skims the artichokes
and rusts the harnesses hanging in stables.
I am the ant guided by constellations
that inhales the odours of land and sea.
A man who dreams himself everything he is not:
the sea damaged by ships,
the black whistle of a train amid bonfires,
the stain that darkens the drum of kerosene.
Though I close my gate before retiring
in my dream it stays open. He who failed to come by day
treading the withered leaves of eucalyptus
arrives at night, certain of finding the way like the dead
who never arrived, yet know my whereabouts
—covered by a shroud, like all those who dream
tossing in the darkness and shouting words
that fled the dictionary and went to inhale the night air
smelling of jasmine
and fermented manure.
Unwanted guests pass through bolted doors and drawn blinds
and stand around me.
Oh mysterious world! No padlock fastens the gate of night.
It was foolish to think that I should sleep alone
protected by the barbed wire that fences my land
and by my dogs who dream with opened eyes.

At night, a mere breeze destroys walls made by men.
Though my gate will be closed by morning
I know that someone has opened it by night
watching me dream restlessly in the dark.

LOSSES AND PRIVATIONS

He who sleeps forfeits the night.
He shuns eternity,
a captive candelabrum
in the darkness of the sky.

He who sleeps forfeits love,
the mature vigil
of the flesh that dreams itself
awakened.

He who sleeps forfeits death
that breathes unseen
like the hare in the forest.

He who sleeps forfeits everything
that fortune places
on the table of the universe.

THE LOST COIN

In my dream I find the lost coin.
It was lying at the bottom of the sea,
in the coral grotto no castaway ever reaches,
in the pure region untouched by death.

When I awake I am as silent as fish.
My land, just like the sea, has the purity of water.
All words are but lost coins.

FIVE PROSE POEMS

MAXINE CHERNOFF

THE SMELL CONVENTION

Like a zoo with only one animal, like a doctor who listens to hearts through a yam, I was a rarity. What was I doing at the smell convention? But I had a civic duty. Who else might testify against lemons, those prissy pouters? Who else might nix nectarines? My sense of smell, acute as bats' radar, was my credential. I wore it on my face like a tear in a flag. I was after the riot of smells that engulfs us in stores, circuses, our own sad bodies. Why, if there were only one smell to cope with, as bland as a nurse, we would be free.

"You can't go on like this," I told the delegate from Utah, spraying himself with essence of the Great Salt Lake. He didn't listen.

"Death to dogwood!" I interrupted the keynote speaker, whose garlic necklace was studded with cough drops.

Oh, they were subtle! Overcome by elixir of Reuben sandwich, I staggered to my chair. It smelled of last week's rainstorm on the fourth green. Where could I hide? Tiny smell-arrows were everywhere!

Trying to remain calm, I slipped on my wetsuit and dove in. I swam in a sea of Girl Scout cookies, dripping batteries, *eau de* key-in-the-lock, sailors' bedsheets.

SPRING

Mrs. Smith takes Mr. Smith in the closet while the children dream in unison of Napoleon. It happens every spring. Spirit pounds flesh, and you think the newsman said "languor." Next door the professor is vibrantly thinking, theories brightening the room at nine P.M. *So*, he sighs, *in this instance the British spelling is correct.* A fruit fly circles over his dictionary. Another battle won. In the nearby church a bell insists in the highest tower. It reminds us of a toothache or nostalgia. Meanwhile, she's ripped her nylons on his limitations. He wears suspenders, the nerve! You close your eyes and point to a map, finding yourself in an Amazon so blue you worry for the ocean. That's the give and take of it, the getting out of yourself at least for a stroll down the Avenue of Busted Cups. It's March 19th, time to slaughter the poinsettia. A white milk oozes from the stem onto the mahogany. The king is dead. If your ideas had form like a milk bottle left on the porch, you'd take them in the closet and caress them. You wouldn't be discreet. You'd understand the implications but finally wouldn't care. After all, this is a poem about love.

MISS CONGENIALITY

Even as an embryo, she made room for "the other guy." Slick and bloody, she emerged quietly: Why spoil the doctor's best moment? When Dad ran over her tricycle, she smiled, and when Mom drowned her kittens, she curtsied, a Swiss statuette. Her teachers liked the way she sat at her desk, composed as yesterday's news. In high school she decorated her locker with heart-shaped doilies and only went so far, a cartoon kiss at the door. She read the classics, *The Glamorous Dolly Madison,* and dreamed of marrying the boy in the choir whose voice never changed. Wedding photos reveal a waterfall where her face should be. Her husband admired how she bound her feet to buff the linoleum. When she got old, she remembered to say pardon to the children she no longer recognized, smiling sons and daughters who sat at her bedside watching her fade to a wink.

HAIRDO

Part avalanche, part retort, it begins inside the unknowing scalp. Pay attention to the symptoms. No matter how even the part, how tight the bun, a hairdo may take residence. Squatters' rights exist beyond the law: try arresting a hairdo. The compelling insistence of the hairdo to a life of its own (witness its growth after death) rivals the legendary tenacity of gold prospectors. The day it is born the will collapses; the mind embraces the change like a convert the picture of his prophet.

It is Tuesday. And the fern that is her hairdo has grown overnight. First she is logical—what did she eat for dinner? what dream? The comb is useless and so is the scarf. So she boards the usual bus for work, beaming randomly at passengers, thankful for their discretion. Not only do they ignore *her* fern but the nun with the shopping bag bangs and the driver with the broccoli coif (strange she never noticed them before). Or is it that only she can detect the change, as the adolescent girl in her dark bedroom touches her breasts, growing like radishes under the skin?

THE UNZIPPED

In these times of boxer shorts depicting steeplechases, we envy the unzipped. Listen, I'm talking to you, children with milk in your mouths and widows who sleep with their clothes on in case of fire. The unzipped are among us. If you ask them their dreams, they'll say *the man who invented swimming* or *castanets over Maui.* You may have spoken to one this morning, that sweaty young man in the drugstore, shameless as the weather. Dare I send you reeling like a migraine? You, stranger, might be married to one. To find out, perform this test. Check into a lousy hotel whose neon sign has shrunk to a twitch. Tell your husband you're going out for a sandwich but return five minutes later. Does he stare at you with the reluctance of a bootblack? Or observe. Does he worship lizards, his nonchalant cousins? Does he lose buttons regularly as you receive junk mail? And what of the burden on the zipped, those commuter train jockeys, those flat on the back sleepers? Isn't it unfair how the unzipped always got away with things? Your sister was one with her slippery childhood, those children who shouted in movies, the pretty teacher who laughed at the jokes of her worst student. Face it: only you are zipped!

FIVE POEMS

SALLY FISHER

ANNUNCIATION GHAZAL

From *Five Paintings*

Mary has a slit in her dress at stomach level
and the bird nose-diving on a beeline right toward it.

Gabriel's elegant bare foot touches her stone floor.
He shivers; he never walked on anything before.

He lands on the porch. Her head's not yet turned but she feels
a draft, loses her place reading, and her breathing jumps.

Her room is tidy. She is beautiful and lost
in thought. Her concentration makes him come. He speaks.

She will close her eyes. He will open the lids on
the other side; they look in, he, she, looks in, out.

DROP EVERYTHING

From an *Annunciation* by Tintoretto

Broken lumber in the back yard. Stucco falls
away from the brick. Inside, straw hangs down

beneath the raveled chair seat, the spinning is
interrupted, laundry all over the place

and mending. A small book has dropped from her hands—
large hands, not meant for needle and thread. The book

will slip from her heavy thigh. She has been trying
to read in these surroundings. Gabriel, arms

reaching out, sails right in the door. Down through the
transom a throng of flying babies streams like

a school of dolphins led by the white dove.
She is bowled over. A silent moment.

The two almost laugh in the humming light. Then
she knows: now nothing can proceed without her.

LOVE WON'T STOP

From the *Annunciation* by Simone Martini

He has left the sky, hungry for earth. The broken
branches in his hands and hair smell of wilderness.

Her chair is inlaid with geometrical stars.
A fluted vase of lilies stands on the marble floor.

He was meant for this errand. She has always tried
to make a heaven. Neither has ever been at home.

His pheasant wings fold back. Her mouth and eyes narrow.
She keeps a thumb in the book. She draws in the gold hem

of her veil to cover her bare neck. Love won't stop.
She is folding inward as the diligent words,

visible, travel the space from the angel's mouth,
passing through the lilies, filling with their fragrance.

POEM IN WHICH I ASK FOR HELP

Today I must pray
to a sensible saint,
a reliable mind.
I call on you, Marianne Moore.
I say Oh Miss Moore you must help me;
in a demented place in my backsliding heart
I still believe
love is a swoon, with music.

I'm on the bus now, reading your book
which the book club sent because
I forgot to check Send
no selection this month
though I should have done
because I already have your collected poems.
You see how unlike one another we are.

I crave composure, deliberately earned perception.
I'm thinking of a large-format photograph—
clean white and deep black, detail in the midtones—
painstakingly composed, properly exposed.

You see I don't fall just in love but into everything.
Even to God I'll say the old line
about the jug of wine, the loaf, you know the rest.
You see how confused it is: sex, religion, groceries
and now this photography metaphor.

But to return to your book,
in the back pages, you take my hand

and we walk up step by step into
what your precise editor calls
a "hitherto uncollected" poem.
We rest a moment, where you say
"Nothing mundane is divine,
Nothing divine is mundane,"
and already I'm arguing with you.

I'm sure you have noticed how
in old photographs, children and dogs,
especially dogs, so often erase themselves,
or part of themselves, by moving.
The small cloud they create, sometimes
transparent, is not a flaw, but
an essence caught, time visible, life, love
and death implied, and perfection as well.
I hope you'll forgive a paraphrase.
Meister Eckhart said, Nothing perfect
is complete, and nothing complete
is ever perfect. He also said we ought to expect
God in all things, evenly.

But you know all this, and still have
the patience, the poise, to hold still
to hold fast, and that's why I've called on you.
Here we are standing mid-poem, and I wanted to ask

and there I go
you can see me
one clear foot
wearing my shoe
the rest a smudge
an arc, a blur.

JAMES BROWN LIVE AT THE APOLLO

For Lee Hyla

I can't tell
but I think he's in love with me.
"Now I want you to know I'm not
singing this song for *myself* now!" he said.
They have to drag him off.
They have to catch him in a net.
They have to throw a blanket over him.
But he makes his way out.
He keeps coming back,
practically eating the microphone,
holding it a carrot in front of him,
looking down at it like an ice cream cone.
They have to knock him down and drag him away from me.

THREE POEMS

JOHN ALLMAN

CLOUDS

1
What is blue but absence? A cool wind. Let there be
shadows that grope on hillsides, that ripple and erase
gray mirrors in small ponds: last night's memory of lightning

the white nerve in its myelin sheath, the sprawled synapse
of the birch that cast caged shadows on the garden. Bright
days strung like beads on a single frequency, hissing by.

Let there be mornings after: hands curling over wet cotton,
a grasp opening as cries of birds burst from the trees,
something bundling from the north, howling towards heat.

2
The empty curve: taut from horizon to horizon,
a stiff canopy. Thunder. As if the sun bowled through
a tunnel in space, and fell, and rose on white-hot wings.

Gray, driven scud: huge knees leaning on earth,
floods filling ravines, trees turgid; black billows
the fumes of flight, as sparrows crash into garage windows.

Once, these forsythia stooped under late, wet snow.
Rain gutters glistened, pulling away from the house. No
words from the ice-world. A blankness in speech like cumulus.

3
That formation of rags, caught by the wind,
fluttering over the pinched river, the gray skin of sea.
You are drawn to a salty medium, this estuary that is

the tide of our pulse, pock-marked by a needling-down
from the surface of stars, the leaking light, a turning
over: the bright sides of particles like scurf

from the moon, a kind of madness, an acid
whiteness. You open like night-blooming narcissus
to great movements, a cracking of sky, uninhabited worlds.

4
Now they are the floating heaps of bleached
dust; vistas temporary between them, where no navigation
takes us through, as if passage opened and closed, the salt

falling from the air, a swell rising beneath us, dark
seething, the hump and glow of furnaces the other side
of steel mills, low mountains. And on they drift: vast

white silhouettes, dampness and ice, the mist of a soft fabric
that clings to the faces of climbers. We hear the hum
of suspension bridges, the gasp of heights, tires hot on macadam.

5
If they merged forever into a concave ceiling:
leaving us gray, etiolated, eyes useless and frosted,
fingertips the only retinas; our reach implying spaces

we have never seen; electrostatic drops warping into
the fluid wavering of gravity. But rain is our inconstant
condition, gone by evening; noctilucent islands

in slow procession below the moon, dreams gaping
among trees; one's own hand translucent; shadows of stones
bulging within one's touch. A silence. Sky the only motion.

LEGEND OF THE MINIATURE ROSE

Frost sometimes fails
where talus accumulates its angle of debris
degrees at a time, the year's steep
hypotenuse between mountain and plain. It was here
that Colonel Rouelt, far from the village,
found the flower no larger than his infant daughter's
soul. Its thorns hardly a prickle,
he dropped to his knees, cradled it, blew on the frail
ember of its mouth. At this height,

beyond shadows of creaking wheels and the heavy breath
of oxen, so close to the tarn,
and cirque and cup of glacial retreat, the clutched hand
turns upward, light slides down the slope
like lateral moraine. But he gathered those roots
to his heart, under layered clothing,
close to his damp heat, where the nipple hardens in
sudden draughts, and hair curls gray;
he imagined a window box in sunlight, his daughter's

first words, the steam of soups,
loam crumbling in the darkness, swollen nodules like pink
knuckles of a tiny grasp. Thus, he descended,
the wind slashing him beyond the sheltering rock, above
the freeze-line, as he thought he heard

the clatter of chamois and mouflon, and stumbled, and gripped
    the sharp stones. He felt that moist breath
under his shirt, the root-pulse, the head drooping that he
    and his children would water for a hundred years.

ON ELLSWORTH KELLY'S SCULPTURES

Can nature be this flat, so frontal, like a wall?
This is the plugged mouth of a tunnel, removed,
bolted to the floor, pure entrance, where body is denied.
It's the memory of ore. The blankness that darkens words.

If light could be poured like molten steel, molded
into plates that curved, held facing the sun,
and aged a thousand years, in salty air,
we'd confront it, learn to harvest wheat, with gray

at our backs. We'd lie thin and wide, heavy
with longing, our spines pulled to earth's magnetic
core. The restless among us would shift in the ground,
dig like triangles, plunge like slats, heave

like slabs over ice. We'd awaken to a slanted sky,
our mouths askew, heaviness in the right side
of our heads. Love would be a roundness dreamt
in the geometry of embrace. Hands forever horizontal.

And when they propped us in museums, the tubular
patrons, the new humanity, the evolved and coinless
breed would walk behind us, speaking gibberish,
as we grew sad and stiff: such chill not unhappiness,

but reduction, lost heat, where sides disappear.
They'd bring everyone on line up front, huddled
behind our faces, particular lives melding
to touch the universal surface. Anonymity the perfect art.

AT THE DEATH OF KENNETH REXROTH

ELIOT WEINBERGER

It's a typical story: I was assigned, at my suggestion, to write an obituary on Kenneth Rexroth for *The Nation*, a magazine he had served for fifteen years as San Francisco correspondent. Written in the week after his death, the article was promptly rejected for "overpraising a minor writer"—and a "sexist pig" to boot. (In its place the magazine ran a lengthy piece on some sad flake from the Andy Warhol crowd.) The obituary was then sent, at the recommendation of Carol Tinker, Rexroth's widow, to the *American Poetry Review*. Two months later they replied that they would be happy to run the piece next year, and would I please send a photograph of myself to accompany it? Considering their leisure, and my mug, inappropriate to the occasion, I withdrew the article. *Sulfur* magazine, just going to press, offered to add an extra page in the front of their next issue—and there, in the obscure and sometimes honorable domain of the little magazine, is where a condensed version of my small notice of Rexroth's death finally saw print.

It's a typical story: One cannot even publish an obituary for an American poet, for the best of them die even more forlorn than they lived. In the last twenty-five years, despite the so-called "poetry boom" and the thousands of poetry books published yearly, most of the important American poets have died with most of their work unpublished or out of print. Louis Zukofsky,

H.D., Langston Hughes, Paul Blackburn, Charles Olson, Marianne Moore, Mina Loy, Frank O'Hara, Charles Reznikoff, Jack Spicer, Lorine Niedecker, to name a few. The small group who died in print were either approved by the English Department in their lifetimes (Frost, Eliot, Cummings) or they had the fortune to be published (and kept in print) by New Directions (Williams, Patchen, Pound, Merton, and now Rexroth).

With certain exceptions, the death of an American poet inverts the reputation. Those who were heavily laureled in their lifetimes seem to vanish from their graves. Think of Tate, Ransom, MacLeish, Van Doren, Schwartz, Bogan, Jarrell, Aiken, Winters, Hillyer, and so many more. (And soon to be joined, I suspect, by Lowell, Berryman, Bishop.) For those who were dismissed or neglected in life, death becomes the primary condition for immortality. The English Department is usually too late for the funeral, but they are enthusiastic exhumers. Their critical apparatus grinds into motion and, often many years later, buoyed by exegesis, the original rises to the surface once more. Canonization is complete, and we all too easily assume that those islands were always on the map. (We've already forgotten that Williams won his only Pulitzer Prize posthumously, that the last volume of the *Cantos* was deemed unworthy of review anywhere, that H.D. at her death was remembered only for a handful of her earliest poems and that it took over 20 years for an edition of her *Collected Poems* to appear, that Marianne Moore's *Collected* was, until recently, out of print for seventeen years.)

Now, with a special issue of *Sagetrieb* ("A Journal Devoted to the Poets in the Pound-Williams-H.D. Tradition" published by the University of Maine at Orono) the ivy gates are opening to admit Mr. Rexroth. People will make a living explaining him, and the mountains of his life and work will swarm with curiosity-seekers, pedants, muckrakers and axe-grinders, all as tiny as the figures in a Chinese landscape painting. It's easy to imagine what Rexroth would have said about them—but what will they make of Rexroth? How will they take the most readable American poet of the century and render him difficult—that is, requiring explication, better known as "teachable"?

I sit with a pile of clippings: *Poetry* magazine, reviewing Rexroth's first book, comparing the poems to the license plates made by convicts, and suggesting that the poet consider another profession. Alfred Kazin calling him an "old-fashioned American sorehead." *The New Yorker,* with its usual bemused condescension, nicknaming him "Daddy-O." John Leonard in the *New York Times:* "He lives in Santa Barbara, Calif., where he professes Buddhism and meditates. Meditates? The heart sinks. If Mr. Rexroth is meditating, then he is not being the curmudgeon of old, of fond memory . . . [the] father figure to the various dandies with black fingernails."

And the obituaries: in New York, "Father Figure to Beat Poets"; in L.A., "Artist and Philosopher." A few days later, the longer assessments: Colman McCarthy, in the *Washington Post,* surprised that the newspaper obituaries "ran no longer than a few inches," but assuming that the "magazines that Rexroth wrote for—*The Nation, Commonweal, Saturday Review, Poetry*—[will] provide the full appreciations that he deserves." (None did.) Herbert Mitgang, in the *New York Times* declaring with parenthetical snideness that he "will probably be remembered as a public personality and as an inspiration (in some circles) more than as a major poet, critic or painter."

Born in another country, Rexroth would have served as the intellectual conscience of the nation: a Paz, Neruda, MacDiarmid, Hikmet. But here, as he wrote, "There is no place for a poet in American society. No place at all for any kind of poet at all." So in his life, and at his death, he was largely seen as a crank, a colorful American eccentric who once spiced occasional magazine copy and three well-known romans-a-clef.

It is depressing that a few moments from that vast and protean life were bottled and preserved for use *ad infinitum* whenever the name of Rexroth was mentioned. How sad that he died, in the mind of America, an aged Beatnik. For what is more remote than the Beat Generation? To read *The Dharma Bums* today (where Rexroth appears as a "bow-tied wild-haired old anarchist fud," and which has dated far more than, say, Henry Miller) is to see that the Beats mainly offered an attractive selection of alternative consumer choices—red wine, Chinese food eaten with chopsticks, heterosexual sex without marriage, hitchhiking, a taste for nonrepresentational painting and jazz, occasional tolerance for gay sex, casual dress, some dabbling in meditation and Oriental philosophy and the occult, facial hair, marijuana—all of which quickly became the common stuff of middle-class American weekends while, ironically, the Beats continued to retain their "wild Boho" image.

Rexroth briefly embraced the Beats (despite his famous disclaimer, "An entymologist is not a bug") as he had so many movements: the Wobblies, the John Reed Clubs, anarchism, the Communist Party (which refused him membership), civil rights, the hippies, feminism—most of which posed a far more serious threat to institutional America than the Beats. But as a political thinker and activist, he essentially belonged to "the generation of revolutionary hopelessness." More than any other poet, Rexroth's work records that history of disillusionment: the massacre of the Kronstadt sailors, Sacco and Vanzetti, the Spanish Civil War, the Hitler-Stalin pact, Hiroshima, the Moscow Trials. He wrote, in 1957:

> We thought we were the men
> Of the years of the great change,
> That we were the forerunners
> Of the normal life of mankind.
> We thought that soon all things would
> Be changed, not just economic
> And social relationships, but
> Painting, poetry, music, dance,
> Architecture, even the food
> We ate and the clothes we wore
> Would be ennobled. It will take
> Longer than we expected.

Still he clung to the vision of brotherhood exemplified by the various American Utopian communities whose history he wrote. His 1960 essay, "The Students Take Over," was dismissed by an academic critic as "mad" for "announcing a nationwide revolution among students on behalf of national and international integrity." Yet by 1969 *The Nation* would write, "What is most viable in the so-called New Left is in large part the creation of Rexroth and Paul Goodman whether the movement knows it or not." As always in Rexroth's life, the initial reaction stuck while the fact that he was proved right was forgotten: "When a prophet refuses to go crazy, he becomes quite a problem, crucifixion being as complicated as it is in humanitarian America."

His enemies were the institutions (the U.S. and Soviet states, the corporations, the universities, the church) and their products: sexual repression, academic art, racism and sexism, the charmlessness of the bourgeoisie, the myth of progress, the razing of the natural world. He was an early champion of civil rights, and his essays on black life in America are among the few from the period that have not dated. He was the first poet whose enthusiasm for tribal culture was not picked up from Frazer, Frobenius or the Musée de l'Homme, but rather from long periods of living with American Indians. And he was—almost uniquely among the WASP moderns—not only *not* anti-Semitic, but an expert on Hassidism and the Kabbalah.

Most of all, he was America's great Christian poet—a Christianity, that is, which has rarely appeared in this hemisphere: the communion of a universal brotherhood. And he was America's—how else to say it?—great American poet. For Rexroth, alone among the poets of this century, encompasses most of what there is to love in this country: ghetto street-smartness, the wilderness, populist anti-capitalism, jazz and rock & roll, the Utopian communities, the small bands at the advance guard of the various arts, the American language, and all the unmelted lumps in the melting pot.

As a poet, he had begun with "The Homestead Called Damascus," a philosophical dialogue and the only poem worth reading by an American teenager, and then veered off the track into a decade of "Cubist" experiment. Had he remained there—like say, Walter Conrad Arensberg—he would be remembered as a minor Modernist, less interesting than Mina Loy and far inferior to his French models, Reverdy and Apollinaire. But by the publication of his first book, *In What Hour*, in 1941, Rexroth had abandoned the Cubist fragments of language—while retaining the Cubist vision of the simultaneity of all times and the contiguity of all places—to write in a sparsely adorned American speech. ("I have spent my life striving to write the way I talk.") It was a poetry of direct communication, accessible to any reader, part of Rexroth's communitarian political vision, and personal adherence to the mystical traditions of Christianity (the religion of communion) rather than those of the East (the religions of liberation).

The poetry: political, religious, philosophical, erotic, elegiac;

celebrations of nature and condemnations of capitalism. His long poems of interior and exterior pilgrimage are the most readable in English in this century. Though he wrote short lyrics of an erotic intensity that has not been heard in English for 300 years—worthy of the Palatine Anthology or Vidyakara's *Treasury*—he essentially belonged to the tradition of chanted poetry, not to lyric song. For some critics the poems were musically flat, yet William Carlos Williams claimed that "his ear is finer than that of anyone I have ever encountered." The way to hear Rexroth is the way he read: to jazz (or, in the later years, koto) accompaniment. The deadpan voice playing with and against the swirling music: mimetic of the poetry itself, one man walking as the world flows about him.

Curiously, his effect on poetry in his lifetime was not as a poet, but as a freelance pedagogue and tireless promoter, as energetic and inescapable as Pound: organizer of discussion groups and reading series and radio programs; responsible for bringing Levertov, Snyder, Rothenberg, Tarn, Antin, Ferlinghetti and others to New Directions; advocate journalist, editor and anthologist. Though Gary Snyder can be read almost as a translation of Rexroth; though it is difficult to imagine Allen Ginsberg's "Howl" without the example of "Thou Shalt Not Kill"; though everyone has read the Chinese and Japanese translations; it seems that few, even among poets, have read "The Phoenix and the Tortoise," "The Dragon and the Unicorn," "The Heart's Garden, The Garden's Heart," "On Flower Wreath Hill," or more than a scattering of the short poems.

The result is that Rexroth at his death was among the best known and least read of American poets. It is a sad distinction that he shares, not coincidentally, with the poet he most resembles, Hugh MacDiarmid. (I speak of MacDiarmid's reputation outside of Scotland.) Except for MacDiarmid's orthodox Marxism and Rexroth's heterodox Christianity, which are mutually exclusive, both were practitioners of short lyrics and long discursive and discoursive poems, both were boundless erudites, and both are formed out of the conjunction of twentieth-century science, Eastern philosophy, radical politics, heterosexual eroticism, and close observation of the natural world. (The resemblance, strangely, went beyond intellectual affinity: Rexroth claimed that he was often mistaken for MacDiarmid in the streets of Edinburgh.)

I suspect that the neglect of Rexroth and MacDiarmid is due to the fact that both are, at heart, outside of (despite their varying sympathies for) the "Pound-Williams-H.D. tradition." Their spiritual grandfathers were Wordsworth and Whitman: the life of the mind on the open road. (It is, by the way, how one writes the Chinese *tao:* the character for "head" over the character for "road.") MacDiarmid may have been sunk by his galactic vocabulary, but Rexroth? One guess is that Rexroth was ignored because, by writing poetry that anyone who reads can read, he subverted the system, the postwar university-literary complex. Poets, especially the advance guard, driven to the fringes of society, have developed an unspoken cultishness: a secret fidelity to the "unacknowledged legislator" myth and a tendency toward private languages that are mutually respected rather than shared. The university professors, for their part, enjoy the power of ferreting out the sources and inside information, being the holders of the keys and the decoder rings—playing George Smiley to the poet's Karla. Rexroth blew the circuits by presenting complex thought in a simple language. The English Dept. has no use for "simple" poets, and the Creative Writing School no use for complex thought. He remained an unpinned butterfly.

Nevertheless, there is no question that American literary history will have to be rewritten to accommodate Rexroth, that postwar American poetry is the "Rexroth Era" as much (and as little) as the earlier decades are the "Pound Era." And it will have to take into account one of the more startling transformations in American letters: that Rexroth, the great celebrant of heterosexual love (and for some, a "sexist pig") devoted the last years of his life to becoming a woman poet.

He translated two anthologies of Chinese and Japanese women poets; edited and translated the contemporary Japanese woman poet Kazuko Shiraishi and—his finest translation—the Sung Dynasty poet Li Ch'ing-chao; and he invented a young Japanese poet named Marichiko, a woman in Kyoto, and wrote her poems in Japanese and English.

The Marichiko poems are particularly extraordinary. The text is chronological: in a series of short poems, the narrator longs for, sometimes meets, dreams of and loses her lover, and then grows old. Although Marichiko is identified as a "contemporary woman," only two artifacts of the modern world (insecticide and pachinko games) appear in the poems; most of the imagery is pastoral and the undressed clothes are traditional. The narrator is defined only in relation to her lover, and of her lover we learn absolutely nothing, including gender. All that exists is passion:

Your tongue thrums and moves
Into me, and I become
Hollow and blaze with
Whirling light, like the inside
Of a vast expanding pearl.

It is America's first Tantric poetry: through passion, the dissolution of the world (within the poem, the identities of the narrator and her lover, and all external circumstances; outside the poem, the identity of Marichiko herself) and the final dissolution of passion itself:

Some day in six inches of
Ashes will be all
That's left of our passionate minds,
Of all the world created
By our love, its origins
And passing away.

The Marichiko poems, together with the Li Ch'ing-chao translations, are masterworks of remembered passion. Their only equal in American poetry is the late work of H.D., "Hermetic Definition" and "Winter Love"—both writers in their old age, a woman and a man as woman. Man as woman: a renunciation of identity, a transcendence of self. As Pound recanted the *Cantos* and fell into silence; as Zukofsky ended *"A"* by giving up the authorship of the poem; Rexroth became the *other*.

Pound left us, in Canto 120, with a vision of paradise and the despair of one who cannot enter paradise. Zukofsky left us with a black hole, *80 Flowers*, an impossible density that few will ever attempt to penetrate. And now Rexroth, speaking through the mask of Li Ch'ing-chao, has left us with passion and melancholy, the ecstasies of one woman (man) in a world seemingly forever on the verge of ruin:

Red lotus incense fades on
The jeweled carpet. Autumn
Comes again. Gently I open
My silk dress and float alone
On the orchid boat. Who can
Take a letter beyond the clouds?
Only the wild geese come back
And write their ideograms
On the sky under the full
Moon that floods the West Chamber.
Flowers, after their kind, flutter
And scatter. Water after
Its nature, when spilt, at last
Gathers again in one place.
Creatures of the same species
Long for each other. But we
Are far apart and I have
Grown learned in sorrow.
Nothing can make it dissolve
And go away. One moment,
It is on my eyebrows.
The next, it weighs on my heart.

NOTES ON CONTRIBUTORS

JOHN ALLMAN is the author of two books of poetry: *Walking Four Ways in the Wind* (Princeton University Press) and *Clio's Children* (New Directions). A new collection, *Scenarios for a Mixed Landscape,* is forthcoming from New Directions in 1986.

ALAN M. BROWN is currently working on a novel, *Mystery Man with Twenty-One Faces.* His short stories have appeared in *New Directions 47, California Quarterly,* and other publications.

Born in Chicago in 1927, PAUL CARROLL lives there with his wife, the sculptor Maryrose Carroll, and his son Luke. He was editor of *Big Table* in 1959–61. Since 1969 he has been a professor of English at The University of Illinois in Chicago. Books include: *Odes* (1968), *The Poem in Its Skin* (1968), *The Luke Poems* (1971), and *New and Selected Poems* (1979).

HAYDEN CARRUTH is the author of seventeen books of poetry (including *For You, From Snow and Rock, from Chaos,* and the recently released *Asphalt Georgics,* all published by New Directions). He is presently a professor of English at Bucknell University.

MAXINE CHERNOFF's poetry books include *New Faces of 1952* (Ithaca House), *The Last Aurochs* (Now Press), *A Vegetable Emergency* (Beyond Baroque Foundation), and *Utopia TV Store* (Yellow Press). She also writes fiction, which has appeared in *Fiction, Triquarterly, Iowa Review, The North American Review, Playgirl,* and many other magazines.

The Danish author INGER CHRISTENSEN, a member of the Danish Academy, lives in Copenhagen, dividing her time between writing, editing, and raising her eleven-year-old son. SUSANNA NIED has translated four of Inger Christensen's books of poetry.

INGEBORG DREWITZ, author of radio plays, novels, and short stories, lives in Berlin. Her best known novel is *Gestern war heute—hundert Jahre Gegenwart.* CLAUDIA JOHNSON lives in Austin, Texas. "The News" is her first published translation.

Born in Holland in 1939, RIEMKE ENSING migrated to New Zealand at the age of twelve and now teaches English literature at the University of Auckland. Her works include *Letters—Selected Poems* (Lowry Press), *Making/Inroads* (Coal-Black Press), and *Topographies* (Prometheus Press).

DEBORAH FASS, a Californian, presently lives in Japan, where she is studying at Oita University and teaching English.

SALLY FISHER grew up in Illinois but now lives in New York City, working in publications at The Metropolitan Museum of Art. Her work has appeared in *Field, Shenandoah, Broadway Boogie, Free Inquiry, Poetry East,* and other magazines.

Available collections by the British poet JONATHAN GRIFFIN *are Outsing the Howling* (Permanent Press), *The Fact of Music,* and *Commonsense of the Senses* (Menard Press). His translations include work by Camoẽs, Char, Claudel, Gary, Hoffmansthal, Kleist, and Pessoa (*Selected Poems,* Penguin).

In addition to his *Of the Great House: A Book of Poems* and *The Woman on the Bridge Over the Chicago River,* a new collection of ALLEN GROSSMAN's work will soon be available from New Directions.

LÊDO IVO is one of Brazil's most prolific and witty authors. He has written fifteen volumes of poetry, two collections of short stories, ten volumes of essays, and two novels (including *Snakes' Nest,* New Directions, 1981). GIOVANNI PONTIERO teaches at The University of Manchester; he is at present translating a trilogy of works by Clarice Lispector for Carcanet Press.

"Brother Wolf" is from a forthcoming collection of short fiction by HAROLD JAFFE, who teaches at San Diego State University and is also the editor of *Fiction International.*

Born in Hammersmith in 1933, B. S. JOHNSON lived all his life in London, where he married and had two children. In a brief but productive career (he died in 1973), Johnson was recognized as the most original of the English experimental writers of his generation. His novel *Christie Malry's Own Double-Entry* has just been reissued by New Directions.

JAAN KAPLINSKI was born in 1941 in Tartu, Estonia. A structural and mathematical linguist, his forthcoming *The Same Sea in Us All* (Breitenbush Books) is his first book of poetry translated into English. SAM HAMILL, poet, Sinologue, and co-publisher of Copper Canyon Press, is presently collaborating with Jaan Kaplinski on yet another volume of the author's poems.

Poems by CARL LITTLE have appeared in *The Hudson, The Georgia,* and *The Worcester Reviews.*

Born in Antwerp in 1926, OSCAR MANDEL settled in the U. S. in 1941. He is a professor of English at the California Institute of Technology. *The Book of Elaborations,* his collection of sixteen essays, among them "From Chihuahua to the Border," has just been published by New Directions.

MICHAEL MCCLURE'S *Selected Poems* is forthcoming from New Directions, publisher of many of his books, poetry (*Antechamber and Other Poems, Fragments of Perseus, Jaguar Skies, September Blackberries*) as well as plays (*Gorf, Josephine: The Mouse Singer*).

JOYCE CAROL OATES is a renowned and prolific author of poetry, short stories, novels, and nonfiction. *Marya: A Life,* her newest novel, will be published in January 1986 by Dutton.

Born in Havana in 1939, JUANA ROSA PITA left Cuba in 1961 and has since lived in Madrid, Washington, Caracas, and Miami. In

1975 she was awarded the First Prize of Poetry for Latin America from the Instituto de Cultura Hispánica of Málaga, Spain. She has published several books and in 1985 received the International Prize *Ultimo Novecento* for the totality of her poetic work.

OMAR S. POUND's *Arabic and Persian Poems* was published by New Directions in 1970. His own first volume of poems, *The Dying Sorcerer,* appeared early this year. With A. Walton Litz, he edited *Ezra Pound and Dorothy Shakespear: Their Letters 1909–1914* (New Directions, 1984).

The Collected Prose of CARL RAKOSI came out last year from The National Poetry Foundation, and his *Collected Poetry* is forthcoming. Also available are *Amulet* and *Ere-Voice* (Black Sparrow), and *Droles De Journal* (Coffee House).

JEREMY REED lives in London. His most recent collection of poems, *By the Fisheries,* was brought out by Jonathan Cape Limited.

Born in 1947, HOWARD STERN is a writer and collagist who teaches German at Yale University.

One of the foremost writers of Sweden, GÖRAN TUNSTRÖM has published many volumes of poetry, some novels, and numerous radio plays. Although Tunström's work has been translated into several languages, very little as yet has been published in English. EVA ENDERLEIN is Swedish but has resided in the U. S. since 1969. EMILE SNYDER was born in France, emigrated to the U. S. in 1941, and teaches at Indiana University.

JAMES L. WEIL, publisher of Elizabeth Press, has a new book of poems, *Houses Roses,* forthcoming from Sparrow Press.

ELIOT WEINBERGER lives in New York City and has recently translated Borges' *Seven Nights* and edited Paz's *Selected Poems* (New Directions). He is at work on *The Collected Poems of Octavio Paz,* expected in 1987 from New Directions.